WIRED HARD

A PARADISE CRIME NOVEL

TOBY NEAL

WIRED HARD

A PARADISE CRIME NOVEL

TOBY NEAL

Wired Hard
Copyright © Toby Neal 2017
http://tobyneal.net/

ISBN: Electronic: 978-0-9973089-4-5
ISBN Print: 978-0-9973089-5-2

Cover Design: Jun Ares aresjun@gmail.com
Format Design: Author E.M.S.

Chapter 1

Surveillance work was nine parts boredom and one part terror, Sophie had heard. The boredom part was certainly true. Security specialist Sophie Ang sat back in the creaky office chair and swiveled a bit, working a hand exerciser as she watched three video monitors, each covering a corner of the roughly rectangular former baseball field that hid the buried royal Hawaiian archeological site of Kakela on Maui.

The grainy video feed, exposure turned up as much as possible to counteract the darkness, revealed nothing much of interest. The flat expanse of field, still dimpled with the markings of its years as a baseball diamond, was surrounded by an eight-foot, low-budget chain link fence. The only illumination came from the tired amber glow of a nearby streetlight.

After only three hours in front of the monitors, Sophie wished that the Hui to Restore Kakela, the nonprofit that owned the site, had just hired a night watchman instead of Security Solutions' expensive services.

She put her feet up on the desk and leaned back to stretch, abruptly losing her balance as the old chair tipped.

That woke her up. Too bad the Hui had decided that her partner Jake Dunn was too expensive to afford; she could have used the company—it wasn't easy to fall asleep around Jake.

Glancing one more time at the monitors, Sophie picked up her phone, texting Connor Remarkian. *"This Maui job is very boring. They told me thieves were after priceless artifacts concealed on a buried royal island. It sounded so exciting at the planning meeting on Oahu, but so far, all the job has been is putting in a surveillance system and watching an old baseball field. A lot of unnecessary sitting around."*

Sophie hit *Send.* She was rationing her communication with the man she was seeing, her natural caution balancing the increasing chemistry between them. They'd had their first official date only a week ago—a trip to the Bishop Museum to study up on Hawaiian relics in preparation for this job.

Connor was still recovering from a gunshot wound that had happened during her last case, but had been more than willing to lean on her as they navigated the Bishop's floors of beautifully displayed, well-organized artifact exhibits. Discovering more about how intelligent and well-read he was, not to mention his quick sense of humor, continued to attract Sophie. She wasn't just a person of the body…though his was stellar.

She smiled, remembering photos he'd sent her of him working out—they shared that interest, too.

Connor texted back. *"I was wondering how it was. What did you set up to catch the thieves?"*

"I have motion activated lights, video surveillance, and a big flask of tea to keep me going." She unscrewed the thermos and took a sip, glancing at the monitors again. Still nothing.

"Sounds pretty basic. Why don't they just have a night watchman?"

"I asked the same thing. Apparently, there are security concerns within the organization. Intrigues behind closed doors.

The archaeologist who spearheaded hiring me hinted at internal politics. There is concern that..."

One of the sensor lights turning on in the far corner of the field hurt her eyes with brilliance as it blasted on. Sophie slid the phone with its uncompleted text into her pocket and jumped to her feet, reaching for the Taser at her hip. The rusty old office trailer had been parked in the corner of the Kakela site for so many years that it had become a fixture. She pushed open the metal door and, scanning the empty field, trotted toward the light, holding the Taser in a ready position.

No more serious weapons than that were authorized by the Hui on this job, and she missed the familiar deadly weight of her Glock.

Nothing. The white glare of the light reduced the field to a flat expanse of soft, silty soil and bunchy grass around a baseball diamond area.

Directly beneath the light, at the corner of the fence, a black cat, its eyes a glowing flash, jetted away between some bushes.

Sophie re-holstered the Taser. *It was going to be a long night.* She walked the perimeter of the property, checking the camera angles through a connecting app on her phone.

She reached the corner where active excavation was occurring, and lifted one corner of a large piece of plywood concealing the ruler-straight, five-foot deep rectangular excavation hole, one of several around the site. The orientation tour she had been given with the archaeologist, Brett Taggart, her liaison with the Hui, had been informative about the site's origins and importance.

Taggart looked older than his thirty-six years, with a hatchet face and cynical dark eyes, a cigarette perpetually dangling at his lip. The curved shoulders of an academic were counterbalanced by the sun-bronzed muscles of an outdoorsman, and Taggart wore an Indiana Jones-style fedora with a pair of mirrored aviators and lug-soled boots when he met her at the site to show her around. "What's the good of being an archaeologist if you can't play the part?" he said, when she commented on his outfit.

The Hui nonprofit was slowly excavating the site, which had once been a sacred, royal island with a brackish lagoon surrounding it. Around the turn of the century, the lagoon had been filled in with dirt removed from road construction, an attempt to control mosquitoes that were breeding there as the site fell into ruin.

Taggart had pointed out the area she was now observing. "We're surveying all around the original island site—we aren't as interested in the fill dirt where the lagoon used to be. We took ground penetrating radar images of the entire site, and have begun excavation as the Hui can afford it, in the areas that seem to be of the greatest archaeological significance."

"So what could be so valuable that thieves are trying to steal it?" Sophie asked. "The Hawaiians didn't use gold, or precious gems. I don't know a lot about archaeology, so what makes an artifact valuable?"

"An artifact becomes valuable because of its rarity and cultural significance. Its collectability is also a factor, especially in the private market."

"You mean the black market."

Taggart met her eyes, and his gaze, dark as ale, was sharp and intelligent. "There are plenty of legitimate relics already in circulation that can be bought, sold, and collected. But yes. The black market exists. And that's what we're talking about here. The main items we think these thieves are looking for are human bone hooks."

"Human bone hooks?" Sophie scrunched her brows.

Taggart settled back on his heels, broad, work-roughened

hands dangling between his knees. He took off his hat and pushed a rumpled handful of dark hair off his forehead. "Hawaiians made fishing hooks out of bone and shell. And as you may know, they believed in a connection with their ancestors. *Mana*, the spiritual power that inhabits all things, was believed to be concentrated in the bones of a person. So, sometimes, after an ancestor had been buried and the skeleton was exposed, they would retrieve a bone from an ancestor and carve fishing hooks from it. These hooks were sacred, infused with the *mana* of their ancestors and believed to be good luck, blessed if you will, for the fishing that was so much a part of their survival."

"So did you identify a lot of human bone hooks buried in this site?"

"The GPR isn't strong enough to find items that small, but we've found two so far during our excavations. Each of them is valued at a couple of hundred thousand. Their actual value is priceless, and considered more because Kakela was *kapu*, for royalty only, so the bone they are made of is that of *ali`i*, Hawaiian royalty, and thus even more valuable."

Sophie, hands on her hips, gazed around at the tattered baseball field. "Kind of incredible that no one, back when they filled this place in, understood the significance of it."

Taggart clapped his hat back on his head and stood up. "That's colonialism for you. But picture how it was: a sheltered brackish lagoon filled with fish for eating. The sacred royal palace *hales* on the island in the middle, for living—and some partying." Taggart bounced his brows suggestively. "There were what my mama would have called…goings-on."

"Really." Sophie shook her head. "It's hard to imagine."

"Well, of course all that was gone, broken down, by the time they were building roads and needed somewhere to put the fill dirt. The mosquitoes were bad in the lagoon, which had lost its circulation, so it was a practical solution at the time."

Sophie felt a chill finger of wind zip down her spine and she dropped the plywood back over the hole. She still wasn't sure why the Hui couldn't make do with a night watchman. Taggart had hinted at internal security concerns when he hired her on behalf of the Hui, but hadn't told her what those concerns were.

Life in the private sector was very different from being an FBI agent. As an agent, she had perennially been overwhelmed by a demanding stream of cases, and even when there was a break in the pace, she always had a backlog of long-term projects to work on.

But as a private sector security specialist, her priority was getting and keeping the jobs that Security Solutions assigned to her—no matter how boring—and making sure the security firm had happy customers.

Sophie walked back to the trailer as the sensor light finally extinguished on its timer.

She removed her phone and set it on the desk in front of the monitors. Somehow the text she'd begun to Connor had been erased, and she didn't feel like resuming the conversation. Keeping an eye on the monitors, Sophie rolled out her padded mat and went through a familiar yoga routine, stretching, bending, strengthening. The practice was a central part of her recovery from her early, abusive marriage.

Doing her practice kept her going for a while, but two hours later, she was nodding off again when the sensor light lit up once more.

This time, a figure was clearly visible in the monitor, climbing the exterior of the fence. The sensor light caught him in its blinding illumination, frozen on the fence like a fly caught in a web.

She needed to capture him outside the fence before the sensor light scared him off. Always dressed for action in yoga pants, a sports bra, and athletic shoes, Sophie was already outside and running. She dodged through the unlocked gate beside the trailer, pouring on speed as she ran along the outside of the fence, scanning for the climbing figure.

Of course, the intruder was gone by the time she reached the brightly lit area, but the barking of a nearby dog brought her attention around to the burglar's direction, and she sprinted toward the sound.

The Kakela site was located in the middle of Lahaina town, surrounded by congested residential streets and the beginning of the shopping area of Front Street. The thief was barreling through residential backyards, if the barking of neighborhood dogs was any indication.

Sophie ran as fast as she could, given the obstacles in her way: parked cars, trash cans, a child's plastic wagon. Fences pushed her back into the battered street, and she stepped in a muddy chuckhole, sprawling full length on the worn asphalt.

"Twin snakes conjoined at birth!" Sophie cursed in Thai, rising to her knees, looking at her scraped hands in the yellow glare of the streetlight. She rose slowly, still looking for the thief, and retrieved the Taser that had flown from her hand.

The intruder was gone, and the sound of dogs marking his passage faded into the dark.

Chapter 2

The king tightened his hand around his cell phone. "Say that again."

"They have some heavy security at the site. I almost got caught." The man still sounded breathless.

"Well, that wouldn't do, would it?" The king kept his voice even with an effort.

"Not that I'd have anything to tell them since you made sure I don't know who you are and have no way to reach you but this burner phone number." A long pause. "Do you want me to keep going after the artifacts? Even though there's surveillance?"

"Yes. I want you to find me as many as you can, in fact. Figure out a way."

"You're the boss. I'll need double, and I expect payment in the usual way."

The king's lips tightened. He tapped his fingertips lightly on the burled koa wood desk before him in annoyance, making a sound like far-off drumming. "That will be acceptable. For your extra trouble."

He ended the call, slid the phone into a drawer, and locked it.

Thick, inky darkness coated the windows—being far from neighbors kept the light pollution down. The king liked being *way out in the country, away from other people, away from the noise and bustle that reminded him that* now *wasn't* then.

He got up and walked over to one of the bookshelf-lined walls, filled with the kind of leather-bound, gold-embossed tomes that told a story of money and time. He felt along the shelf and pushed a hidden button.

A few moments later, he entered his secret place.

Automatic lights came up, a dim glow of overhead spotlights that highlighted his treasures. The king bypassed the seating area: a comfortable armchair with a reading lamp beside it, a place where he liked to sit and contemplate all he had spent a lifetime amassing. But today was not a date for contemplation.

He walked to a metal highboy lined with shallow drawers and pulled out the middle drawer. Inside, nested on black velvet trays, a series of gleaming ivory-colored bone hooks seemed to glow. He flicked on the spotlight overhead so that brilliance lit the tray in his hands.

The king could feel mana suffusing the hooks. The essence of power that filled all things, especially the sacred, rose around him like a fragrance. He could feel the hooks' power, their ancient history, and the hands of ancestors who had carved them as they reached out to him from beyond their graves.

Visiting this chamber never failed to put the king in touch with the past he had not been fortunate enough to experience. He was a man out of time, but he could still experience the ancient power of his Hawaiian forebears.

The collection was still missing a hook made from the bone of his ancestral queen. He would not rest until it was complete.

* * *

Sophie looked around the conference table at the Hui to

Restore Kakela's central meeting room. To her left, Brett Taggart rubbed out an unsanctioned cigarette in a chipped ceramic ashtray. To her right, Pomai Magnuson, director of the Hui, opened a pink, fragrant box of Komoda Bakery malasadas. Beside her, the Hui's treasurer, Aki Long, fiddled with a tablet and stylus, making self-important harrumphing noises in his throat.

Across from them, board president Seth Mano steepled his fingers and leveled a stare at Sophie. Mano wore typical Hawaii business casual: a button-down aloha shirt and chinos. He tapped thick fingers together and then smoothed his shirt down over an incipient potbelly.

"So. Take us through what happened again."

Sophie raised her brows. "I already took you through the intruder's attempted incursion, and it's all in the police report I filed last night. I'm not sure what more you need to hear."

Magnuson handed around paper napkins. "Everyone, take a malasada. Director's orders. Ms. Ang, you look exhausted. Perhaps you need coffee as well."

"I have tea." Sophie tapped the thermos of cold Thai tea she'd sipped on the night before. "But I love these. Thank you." Sophie bit into the greasy, tasty, sugary Portuguese pastry. Her tongue encountered a soft haupia coconut pudding filling. "Oh, I love it when they put the filling inside."

"Not strictly traditional, but a great addition," Magnuson agreed. "When everyone is a little more calmed down by sugar and carbs, we can talk about the situation again."

Mano frowned. He pushed his malasada around on the napkin without eating it. His heavy face, dark with a shadow of a beard even at eight a.m., had a bullying poutiness to it.

"Enough with the niceties. I want to know what is being done to catch these thieves."

"I presented your nonprofit with Security Solutions' detailed security plan. Your board approved it," Sophie said stiffly. "Using that plan, we successfully retarded the efforts of a would-be thief last night. The actual capture of the thief is the province of the Maui Police Department."

"Then why aren't they at this meeting?" Mano demanded.

"I invited them to come when I made the report. I believe that this may not be considered a high-priority case. After all, there is no danger to life and limb, and the MPD is spread pretty thin. But I have a detective friend in the Department I can contact personally if you would like me to try that," Sophie said, already feeling guilty to add one more thing to her friend, Sergeant Lei Texeira's plate—*but Lei would want her to.*

"I think we need to discuss possible motivations for the incursions on the site," Taggart said. He'd munched through a malasada in two bites and now dusted his fingertips off on the napkin. "My contract with the Hui is to identify the perimeter of the buried island. We are halfway through that now, and along the way, have identified a number of possible burials indicated by the ground penetrating radar study."

"Anyone with an interest in the site could get the idea that artifacts might be buried there, but the randomness of the holes suggests they don't even know where the island section is, and digging in the former lagoon isn't likely to yield anything," Magnuson said.

"I would like a look at any more detailed maps you have, including the ground penetrating radar study," Sophie said. "Having an idea of what the thieves might be after will help me set up some more targeted surveillance. In the meantime, since I'm there at night, I think you should hire someone to monitor during the day, in case last night's attempt signals an escalation."

"Your contract is already almost prohibitively expensive," the treasurer complained, dabbing his greasy mouth with a napkin. "We make some money renting space in the parking lot in the corner of the site, but that's got to go a long way." The Hui shared ownership of the archaeological site with another community organization and owned a small, paved, pay-per-stall parking lot in one corner of the area that provided a source of revenue.

"We can work something else out," Magnuson said. "To start, I'll have our office employees take shifts during the day out in the trailer. They should be able to keep an eye on things from there, and still get some work done."

"I need to ask you frankly: are you happy with Security Solutions' surveillance plan and my services?" Sophie addressed her question to Magnuson, who, despite her unassuming manner, was clearly the real power player in the room.

"Yes, thank you, Ms. Ang. We're satisfied. You were able to prevent another attempted incursion on the grounds, and now we should be able to prevent more. We just need to figure out what the thieves are looking for." Magnuson picked up another malasada and took a bite.

Mano cleared his throat and tapped the table with his knuckles, drawing all eyes to his face. "I'm not satisfied. And I answer to the Hui's board. I'm not sure what we should be telling them about what's going on at the site."

"We should be telling them that we have the situation in hand." Magnuson met Mano's eyes squarely, and the air seemed to crackle with the confrontation between the two. "In fact, we don't need to tell them anything, if they don't ask. And I'd appreciate you keeping these matters and discussions confidential—though I suspect that ship has already sailed."

Perhaps these were some of the internal politics that Taggart had referred to when Sophie was hired. She glanced at Taggart, and the archaeologist pushed a hand through his hair and stood up.

"I think we can leave the two of you to prep a statement for the board members if you choose to do so. Ms. Ang and I will go look at the GPR report and topographical maps, make sure she's got all the information she needs."

Mano shook his head, but Magnuson inclined hers in dismissal. The opposing signals seemed to be about how these two did business—in total opposition.

Sophie took her cue from Magnuson and stood, gathering her laptop and the folder containing her notes and the police report. "I'll let you know what my friend at MPD says," Sophie told Magnuson. "Sergeant Texeira may be able to find us some more support in actually capturing the thief."

Chapter 3

Sophie spent another hour with Taggart and then returned to her condo to rest before the night's surveillance shift. Security Solutions had rented her a place at Sugar Beach Condos, a complex on the ocean in Ma`alea near Kahului. She was exhausted, but the thought of lying down in the shabby, impersonal room and trying to sleep didn't appeal. Standing in the unit's kitchen, decorated in the mint-green decor of the late eighties, she pulled her phone out and called Lei.

"Hey girl. You on the island yet?" Lei's familiar voice made Sophie smile. She'd texted that she had a job on the Valley Isle, and to expect a call.

"At my condo now, too wound up to sleep, though I've got a graveyard surveillance shift again tonight. Did you have lunch yet?" Sophie paced in front of the sliders, which gave a view of wind-whipped Ma`alea Bay, Kahoolawe a purple smudge in the light-struck distance. Cutout plastic whales adhered to the windows, interfering with the view.

"Was just going to eat at my desk at the station, but meet me at Ichiban in the Kahului Shopping Center."

Half an hour later, Sophie embraced her friend outside the little hole-in-the-wall Japanese restaurant in Kahului. Lei's curly hair tickled her nose, and her friend felt wiry and petite in Sophie's arms though she was only three inches shorter than Sophie's five foot nine.

"So good to see you. How's Kiet?" Lei and her husband, Michael Stevens, had recently adopted Stevens's son by his first wife, a sweet-natured baby boy that Sophie adored. "Has he begun asking to see Auntie Sophie yet?"

"Ha. He's only six months old! We're happy he's begun to say Da-da." Lei pushed open the glass door with its jingling bell and led the way into the dimly lit restaurant. Dusty rice paper lanterns hung over utilitarian Formica tables decorated with bottles of Aloha Shoyu and metal napkin holders.

"Shows what I know about babies," Sophie said. "He seems so smart. I have to see him while I'm here."

"We'll have you over for family dinner. We do that every Friday. You can flirt with Jared." Lei quirked a brow, showing her dimple. Her husband's younger brother was a single firefighter who enjoyed a variety of ocean sports that kept him in top shape, which Sophie had already noticed. She ducked her head in embarrassment. Jared *was* very attractive, but she'd already decided a long-distance relationship was too difficult with her crazy schedule—*and now, there was Connor.*

The women sat at a table that looked out through a plate glass window covered in a peeling light-proofing film. The view into the parking lot consisted of a battered monkeypod tree, parked cars, and a busy thoroughfare. A window air conditioner wheezed over their table.

Lei caught Sophie's look as she broke apart a pair of wooden chopsticks, and laughed. "The food is good—and cheap." Lei smoothed the light cotton jacket she wore over her shoulder-holstered Glock and pushed errant brown curls behind her ears. Her tilted brown eyes were bright with interest. "Tell me about your case. I've been curious about the Kakela site for a while."

Sophie picked up the laminated menu. "Let's order first." They placed their orders with the waitress and sipped plastic glasses of water. "So. You aren't even going to ask about my face?" Sophie couldn't keep a plaintive note out of her voice as she touched her cheek in a gesture that was becoming habitual. The bone of that cheek was a prosthetic, and the skin graft that had been sewn over it, covering the devastation caused by a gunshot wound, still felt numb and tingly.

"Sophie." Lei grabbed Sophie's hand and pulled it down from her face. Neither of them was a 'toucher,' so Sophie's eyes widened in surprise as her friend gazed at her intently. "I'll be honest. This is one of those situations where I don't quite know what to do or say. You got shot in the face less than two months ago. I was just sick that I couldn't come visit you while you were recovering, but between the baby and work I couldn't get over to Oahu…"

"I know. I wasn't trying to get your sympathy or make you feel bad. I just…"

"No, let me finish. I didn't want to not mention it, because it was such a big thing in your life. It would be in anyone's! But honestly, you look the same to me. I mean, technically you don't—when I look closely, I can see that your eyes are a little off: one's wider than the other, and the skin graft area is a little lighter in color. There's a scar around it…but it just doesn't stand out to me. If anything, your face is more beautiful and interesting now. It hints at stories you have to tell."

Sophie gave a wet chuckle. "Oh, I have stories. But not ones I like to tell." She blinked moisture from her eyes, and Lei let go of her hand. They both tugged napkins out of the dispenser and Sophie dabbed her eyes while Lei blew her nose, and they both laughed self-consciously as the waitress set plastic bowls of miso soup down in front of them.

"I'm still so self-conscious about it—especially with people who knew me before. I met all these new people here for the Maui job and it didn't bother me." Sophie spooned up a mouthful of broth. "I have my last scar removal laser treatment next week and have to fly back to Oahu for it."

"Your doctor did a beautiful job, and I'm not just saying that. I think in a year or so, you'll hardly be able to tell but for that part up in your hairline."

"Well, that's why I'm growing my hair out." Sophie tugged at a handful of thick, dark brown curls. She'd always kept her hair buzzed short for easy care and her MMA fighting hobby, but now it was already three inches long, surrounding her head in a halo of ringlets. The skin graft had extended up into her scalp on the left side, and she arranged her hair to cover it. "So, my case. I had to talk to you about it anyway, so I'm glad you had time for lunch." Sophie filled Lei in on the overview of the thefts at the site, and on her meeting with the three Hui leaders and Taggart. "Taggart gave me some more information after the meeting about where more artifacts may be buried on the island."

"How about I come out and check out the site?" Lei addressed her teriyaki beef with enthusiasm. "I can see the setup, and talk to the boys and make sure Lahaina PD is taking the burglaries seriously."

"Anything you can do would be great." Sophie ate several bites of her tofu stir-fry, then picked up her cup of miso and sipped. "I'd love to be able to tell that arrogant board president Mano that MPD was doing all they could, and that I was part of facilitating that." She described the dynamic within the Hui leadership. "There seems to be internal strife between the head of the board and the director. Thank God Taggart got me out of there today." She took another sip and set the soup down. "It does seem like the thieves are targeting something that they're looking for at the site. Taggart thinks it could be one of Kamehameha's wives' burial site." Sophie scrolled to a note on her phone. "Kanipela was her name. The legend is that she drowned in the lagoon around the sacred island, dragged into the water by a *mo`o*, a Hawaiian water dragon spirit. Taggart thinks there's a good chance she was buried on the royal island, which is where Kamehameha had his royal compound until it was moved to Oahu."

"Even I know that would be quite a coup to discover," Lei said. "You mention this Taggart character a lot. Tell me about him. I'm surprised I haven't met him around the island."

Sophie shrugged. "Different circles, I guess. He's an interesting man. Very knowledgeable." Taggart's dark eyes, flashing with enthusiasm under the brim of his hat, were vivid in her mind from earlier. His hands moved as he acted out the story, describing the legend of the *mo`o* dragging the queen out of her canoe down to her death in the lagoon.

"He attractive?" Lei's sharp eyes never missed a thing.

"Yes. In a rugged sort of way." Sophie shrugged. "He smokes." But smoking wasn't the deal breaker for her that it was for some; she'd grown up around a lot of it overseas, and her father had smoked when she was little. "But I'm dating someone."

"So tell me more about this mystery man you're going out with."

Sophie's cheeks heated. She picked up a piece of tempura with her fingers and busied herself eating for a few moments, calming her heart rate. There was no way Lei knew Connor's secret—her friend was only referring to the fact that she didn't know Sophie's current flame.

"His name is Todd Remarkian. He's the CEO of Security Solutions." Sophie kept her eyes on her plate, dipping a piece of tempura into sauce casually. "He's Australian. A very nice man. Fun. We like to take run-hikes with our dogs."

Lei leaned forward, smiling. The tiny, cinnamon-colored freckles across her nose and cheeks caught the light of the overhead paper lantern. The dimple in her cheek winked. "Dating the boss? Marcella tells me you two are thick as thieves."

"I guess technically Todd is my boss, but it's a big company, and I have a different supervisor." Sophie fiddled with her chopsticks. It was hard to talk about a relationship so new and so full of secrets. So tentative, and yet, already tested by life and death situations. So chaste, yet full of unexpressed passion. Sophie couldn't even bring herself to tell Lei his real name— holding it close felt like a warm ember on a cold night.

Lei sat back, grinning. "I guess I'll just have to wait and see how things develop. I was sorry about you and Alika. That could have been something good. But it was time to get back on the horse, and I'm glad to see you're doing that."

"What is it with Americans and getting on horses?" Sophie picked up a piece of tofu with her chopsticks. "I fail to see the connection between a relationship and horseback riding."

"And if you can't make that mental leap, you've obviously been celibate too long."

This time they both laughed.

Chapter 4

*T*wo nights later, Sophie was sitting in a semi-trance watching the monitors when one of the sensor lights went off, accompanied by a loud banging on the metal gate of the site's fenced enclosure. "Sophie!"

Sophie was already on her feet. She started in surprise at the sight of her partner at Security Solutions, Jake Dunn, in the monitor. His all-black, combat-ready clothing projected an intimidating message, as did his height and build—but his ready grin was pure masculine charm.

Jake was a badass, but also a big softie who loved Ninja Turtle cartoons on Saturday, too much relish on his hotdog, and to give her fashion advice.

Sophie jogged out of the trailer and unlocked the gate to let her partner in, feeling a distinct lift in her spirits. "Jake! What are you doing here?"

Jake swung her up in his arms for a too-long hug. He never really stopped flirting in spite of her many reminders, and after months of working together, she had to admit she wasn't totally averse to it.

Jake kissed her cheek with a resounding smack. "Had to come over to make a pitch for another contract, and couldn't resist breaking up my favorite partner's exciting evening."

"And thank God you did. I was about to disgrace myself by falling asleep again." Sophie pushed against Jake's chest to get him to let go of her. "What job is this?"

"I might as well tell you inside. We can get more comfortable." He bounced his brows, incorrigible.

"Come into my palace." Sophie led him to the dilapidated trailer. "When you told me this was a job at a royal Hawaiian archaeological site, I had something a bit grander in mind."

Jake followed her up the rickety step. Inside, he looked around, hands on hips, overhead light gleaming on short dark hair, highlighting his shoulders in the tight black shirt. "This was not what I was told on the phone. They told me expense account. Air conditioning. A nice condo. We should never take jobs sight unseen—hence my trip over to check out this new one."

"Well, I suppose technically that's all true." Sophie hit the button on the ancient wall AC, and the unit rumbled into life. Condensation dripped into a can set beneath it. "I turned it off because somehow the noise makes me sleepier, and doesn't really do anything temperature-wise."

Jake pulled a folding metal chair over to the desk and sat on it, extending long legs in black combat boots up to the desk's surface and crossing them at the ankle. "Yeah. I was sold a bill of goods on this job. I should have taken it, not you."

"Well, except that I wanted it. I wanted to come see my friend Lei, get a change of scenery. I love Maui. And as for the job, except for the part where I'm a glorified night watchman, the situation at the nonprofit is interesting. It appears the thieves are looking for something specific as they dig these holes." Sophie unlocked one of the desk drawers, and took out a thick report. "This is the interpretation of the ground penetrating radar survey done by the archaeology firm contracted by the Hui to

Restore Kakela. This shows possible burial sites and concentrations of artifacts on the actual island, which is what this trailer is standing on. Most of the field you see out there is a former lagoon filled with dirt from the construction of the road leading out of Lahaina. It is unlikely to have had anything in it that didn't decompose in the water. But the part that is the island..." Sophie unrolled the blue surveyor's map of the site and spread it on the desk for Jake to see. "This island might even hold the burial site of one of Kamehameha's queens."

Jake steepled his thick fingers. "How real is that? Because if it is, that's something that would really put Kakela on the map."

"I don't know how real it is. But, I'm getting to understand a little better what the archaeologists' priorities are." Sophie paged to the section in the report that seemed to indicate possible burials and relics on the island. "The GPR can't distinguish small details, but these shapes indicate a possible buried canoe, which Brett Taggart, the archaeologist I'm working with, seems to think could be the queen's burial site."

"So why hasn't anyone excavated that? It seems like the first thing they would do."

"Dr. Taggart's archaeology firm was hired to survey the site and locate all the edges of the island area. The Army Corps of Engineers is slated to come remove all the fill dirt in the former lagoon area in a few months. Once that is done, restoration of the actual island area will begin. The burial site will likely remain undisturbed. Hawaiian cultural value is to leave the burials the way they were and not excavate them."

"But that could leave the site open to vandals or thieves." Jake frowned. "Which is why Security Solutions is involved at all. Wouldn't finding the queen's burial site increase those problems?"

"Not if no one knew it was found." Sophie traced the oblong

shape of the possible canoe in the report's illustration. "This report is highly confidential. Only the inner circle of leadership at the Hui has access to it. And you're right. That's one of the risks with a specific burial. If they build any sort of marker or monument, it could attract the kind of negative attention they've struggled with in Egypt."

"There's no silver, gold, or precious gems here in Hawaii."

"No, but look at this example." Sophie flicked open pictures on her phone. Pomai Magnuson had shared a photo of a chief's necklace made entirely from polished dogs' teeth. The lei had a hypnotizing, barbaric beauty. "This is a relic that was found on the site of a hotel built here on Maui. The body was reburied with this artifact, and blessed by a *kahu,* priest, on the grounds. It's hidden beneath a rock formation so no one knows where it is. But don't you think this is the kind of thing that a Hawaiiana collector would do just about anything to get his hands on?"

Jake leaned in close to look at the photo on her phone. He pinched his fingers to open it wider, examining the detail of the polished ivory canines. "I see what you mean."

"And here's a drawing of one of the human bone hooks found at this site." Sophie scrolled to the illustration. The bone hook was an arc of the polished, tea-colored bone with holes drilled in the top and bottom. "Taggart told me these are not photographed, in order to show respect."

"Where is the barb to keep the fish on?"

"The Hawaiians were master fishermen. They didn't want a precious bone, infused with the mana of their ancestors, to be broken. Two separate barbs were lashed onto the hook's body with animal hide at the bottom, and they could break off if necessary, from here." Sophie leaned over to point, and heard the soft sound of a deeply indrawn breath—Jake inhaling.

Was he...smelling her?

Sophie pulled back, her neck instantly hot, but Jake continued to look down at the phone as if nothing had happened. She cleared her throat. "So, anyway, I wish there was a picture of a completely restored bone hook that I could show you, but this is an idea of what we're dealing with. The bone is this color because of staining from the surrounding soil."

"I think I have more of an idea about these, and I can see the appeal." Jake looked up at her. "You do any fishing?"

"A little bit when I was a child growing up in Thailand, but nothing since."

"I'll take you sometime. Great way to spend time in nature and bring something home to eat too."

"Sounds fun." *But would he try to turn it into a date?* She'd told him she was seeing someone, but he didn't seem to take the hint—or even the outright slapdown. "Tell me about this job you're here to pitch."

"Shank Miller, a rock star with a beach house in Wailea, has become a part of a kayak tour." Jake leaned back and away, lacing his hands behind his head. "The tour is technically staying outside of the no-harassment zone, but the tourists and paparazzi are camping out on the beach, trying to get a shot of him or his girlfriend sunning naked." Jake reached into his pocket and pulled out a plastic-wrapped rod of beef jerky. "Want some?"

"No, thanks." Sophie sat back down in her chair to watch the monitors as he unwrapped the snack.

"Anyway, Miller wants a full security system and he's had a couple of incursions, so he wants to hire permanent bodyguards to keep the riffraff out of his area. As you know, no one can own Hawaii beaches, so rabid fans are able to get closer to celebrities here than just about anywhere."

"Sounds like you'll be the one with the expense account and the nice condo."

"So far, so good on that score. Open bar and kitchen with a chef in the main house. Miller's putting me up in a 'cottage.'" Jake made air quotes. "It's bigger than our office area on Oahu."

"I take it you're pretty motivated to get the gig."

"Well, I made my best effort today, but there are several firms that sent over reps and estimates, so..." Jake shrugged. "But if Security Solutions gets the job, I'll need a partner."

Staying in a cottage with Jake 24/7 wasn't such a good idea...

"But I'm already busy, so if these two Maui situations overlap, I won't be available."

"Miller's got his mainland security team holding down the fort, and you're only on this Hui contract for two weeks, right? So it could work out. In fact, I'm going to propose to Remarkian that we open a satellite office over here on Maui, since we fly over so much and we both like it here." Jake grinned, but his gunmetal-gray eyes were flinty. "Not that I think Remarkian will let *you* leave Oahu."

"We're dating. Remarkian doesn't own me," Sophie said. "Time for a perimeter check." She stood up, picking up the heavy metal flashlight and Taser. She needed to get a breath away from Jake.

She walked outside of the trailer and deliberately out through the gate, outside of the fenced enclosure and range of the sensor lights. The cool night air, sweet with the smell of plumeria and dust, tickled her nose and calmed her nerves.

Jake just needed to be reminded of boundaries—and that she was halfway in love with someone else.

Connor.

Connor, who could play the violin like a virtuoso, and computers just as well. Connor, who liked to rock climb and scuba dive and run-hike challenging trails with her and their dogs. Connor, who had told her that he loved her, and had taken a bullet to prove it.

Connor, who had a mysterious and deadly alter ego.

Sophie kicked an overripe mango hidden in the leaves under one of the big spreading trees that were so much a part of the Lahaina landscape. She peeked into the screened windows of the small older homes that lined the humble street, enjoying the sight of families seated around dinner tables and televisions. Barking dogs and the soft clucking of chickens, the hiss of a cat, the rustle of the wind in coconut palms—even a humble life in Hawaii was preferable to life anywhere else.

Sophie wasn't sure when that had become true for her, but it was.

When she was good and ready, Sophie returned to the trailer, and the great big presence of Jake Dunn.

"I brought a movie for us to watch. I thought I'd keep you company tonight." Jake had opened the small backpack he'd been carrying. He took out a tablet. "The new Star Wars ought to keep us awake for a few more hours."

"Funny how it never occurred to me that I could be watching anything but the monitors," Sophie said drily.

Jake snorted. "Multitasking. I highly recommend it."

They settled into their chairs, and as the movie got going, Sophie realized how glad she was for the company.

Chapter 5

Sophie got up after a morning nap at her condo to recover from the graveyard shift, and decided it was better for her to see what Jake had to set up in person before she made a decision about working the job with him. She texted him that she was coming, then left the condo in Ma`alaea and headed out, yawning from the late night.

Wailea was an immaculately groomed area of huge houses on the south coast of Maui, hidden from the public eye by high privacy gates and screening rows of ornamental palms. She passed the main hotels, and, following GPS cues, turned down into a small side road that looped along the island's most expensive beach.

Sophie frowned as she pulled up beside a fifteen-foot coral stone wall with a closed metal gate across the front.

Something about the street address was familiar. *She had seen that name and number somewhere.*

Sophie picked up her phone and scrolled through the list she had made of the addresses and contact information for the people and possible witnesses on the case. The Hui's board treasurer, Aki Long, lived right beside Shank Miller's estate.

Sophie craned her neck, but she couldn't see Long's entrance around the palms and the coral stone wall, but it had to be on the right of the Miller estate, according to the street numbering.

Sophie pulled into Shank Miller's estate entrance and leaned over to a black stone obelisk on the left with a recessed security camera and coded buttons.

She pressed the intercom and a tinny female voice spoke. "State your business."

"Sophie Ang, here to see security specialist Jake Dunn." The rounded video dome activated, a brief flash of movement, and the metal gate retracted.

Sophie pulled the car forward into a circular drive that reconnected with the gate so cars could drive through without reversing. She pulled into an apron of parking area planted with ornamental palms, and parked beside Jake's black Ford Escape rental.

Her partner bounded out to meet her with his trademark energetic stride, wearing his usual black. "Sophie! Glad you could make it to check out the scene. Feast your eyes on paradise!"

Sophie locked the door of her rental and followed Jake along a path of lava rocks interspersed with emerald green poufs of moss. The front door of the ocean-facing mansion was double-sided, each heavy panel inset with thousands of pieces of beach glass in a mosaic of waves. Jake took hold of one side of the double doors by a conch shell handle, and gave it a tug.

Inside, the gleam of polished, dark wood floors was counterbalanced by furniture covered in cotton canvas slipcovers decorated with aqua pillows. A bank of glass windows opened to a view of the ocean and beach, with the tiny island of Kahoolawe a violet shadow on the horizon.

Sophie could not restrain a gasp. "This is beautiful."

"Shank is out of town on tour right now. I've been working on improvements around the grounds to put in the equipment we need." Jake led her across the gleaming expanse of room to a sunken seating area. More couches created inviting seating in front of a bank of huge glass sliders.

A tall black woman wearing a Hawaiian print wrap dress approached from the modern, open kitchen area, wiping her hands on a dishcloth. Huge gold hoops almost brushed her shoulders and her close-cropped hair was colored a striking henna. "Welcome to Hale Kai. I'm Antigua, and I keep everything running around here."

Sophie smiled as she shook the woman's hand. "Sophie Ang. I work with Jake, and I love your name."

"Antigua is amazing. This woman can cook like an angel and she's my right-hand woman with the security project." Jake looped an arm around Antigua's shoulder, giving a squeeze. "She pretty much excels at everything." They exchanged a smile that made Sophie blink. *Was her partner involved with this woman?* It was none of her business.

Sophie sat down on the edge of a white couch. "This place has a feel of some of the beautiful ex-pat homes my father took me to visit in Thailand. I can only imagine how much a place like this costs on Maui."

"Well, Shank has the dough. But if you look out the door, you can see our security challenges right away. He doesn't want anything in the way of his view, and that leaves the whole front of the estate open to penetration from the beach." Jake pushed open one side of the sliders and led her out onto an artfully weathered teak deck with steps leading down toward the swath of lawn that ended at the beach. "A Plexiglas wall is already in the works," Jake said. "We'll have a fence then. I'm setting up motion-detecting perimeter alarms today. I had to wait until Shank was out of town for all of these improvements. He hates to be reminded of how vulnerable he is."

"I don't blame him for that." Sophie walked to the edge of the lawn along sandstone pavers sunk into the grass. "So this seems like a big job."

"The initial set up and staffing, yeah. Why I could use help. With just me, it's taking longer. You could put in that nanny cam A.I. program a lot faster than I can, for starters."

The ocean glittered turquoise and cobalt, ruffled by the ever-present breeze. Just beyond the edge of the yard, the beach stretched away, peopled by only a few visitors. Sophie turned to look at the mansion beside them.

Aki Long's mansion was completely different, done in a modern minimalist style of intersecting blocky shapes in cream-colored stucco. A thick ti leaf hedge with wire embedded on the inside encircled it. On impulse Sophie walked out onto the beach and headed to the right.

"Sophie! Where are you going?"

"Just saying hi to our neighbor." Sophie headed for the estate's gate, a gap in the tall ornamental hedge. She knocked on the metal gate, loudly.

Aki Long tugged a logo-decorated golf shirt down over a paunch of belly and ran a hand through thinning salt-and-pepper hair as he came down off a wide white stone porch to speak to her. He was not happy to see her, judging by the way his brows drew together. "Ms. Ang. To what do I owe this unexpected visit?"

"I was just in the neighborhood." Sophie tried an engaging smile. "We are putting together a security package for your neighbor, and I was surprised to see that your home is in this area." She made an arm gesture that encompassed the expensive real estate all around them.

"Being a CPA pays rather well," Long said acidly. "Not that it's any of your business."

Sophie kept up the smile. "Of course. Have you had any security concerns? As we put together our services for your neighbor, it would be a big help to know what kinds of measures have worked for you."

Sophie could almost hear the man thinking, though his blocky face was expressionless. *Should he invite her in, play the host, or would it be better to stonewall her?*

"That information is private and confidential," Long said, with a chilly smile. "How good would my security be if I went around giving out my personal information to anyone who asks?"

Stonewalling it was, then.

Sophie inclined her head. "Well, thanks anyway. It was nice to see you again, Mr. Long."

"Certainly hope you are able to stop those thieves at the Kakela site," Long said. "I'm sure you're doing the best you can."

His tone told her he believed the opposite to be true.

Jake stood in the sand watching the exchange, his hands on his hips, but his brows were drawn together as she returned. "What was that about?"

"Nothing. Just thought I'd say hi to the Hui's board treasurer—he's your next-door neighbor."

"Small island," Jake said. "Follow me and I'll show you the cottage. There are separate bedrooms and everything."

The cottage was small and well-appointed, and it did look like they would have enough privacy to function. On their way back, Antigua brought out a plate of delicious shrimp puffs and melon and prosciutto. "Jake tells me you need a little persuading to take the job. Let me lure you with snacks," the woman said, her teeth gleaming like pearls.

"I do love good cuisine." Sophie loaded up a napkin and popped a bite into her mouth. "Thank you. You are very kind."

Jake filled a big palm with the shrimp puffs. He tossed one into the air and caught it in his mouth. "You make me into a trained seal, Antigua. I'll do anything for your cooking."

Antigua smiled at Sophie. "Does he ever settle down?"

"Not that I know of," Sophie said. "I think he's twelve going on…what is it, Jake? Thirteen?"

"Hey! Sophie made a joke!" Jake clapped her on the back and she staggered. "Antigua, my friend here is frighteningly smart—and literal. I am honored to have provoked her first known attempt at humor."

"English is my second language," Sophie told Antigua. "I'm American and Thai, and I grew up there." She glanced at her phone. "Speaking of friends, I am on my way to share dinner with another friend and her family. I must be going."

Antigua insisted on wrapping up some of the appetizers to take with her, "As a pupu. Never arrive empty-handed in Hawaii!"

Jake walked her back to the cars. "I think this is going to be fun." His gray eyes were sincere.

"It's certainly a more luxurious setting than my current one," Sophie agreed. "See you soon."

After Jake let her out of the estate, Sophie drove her rental car out to Lei and Stevens's compound in Haiku on the east shore of Maui. She yawned—that early morning nap she'd taken hadn't done much to restore her energy.

The Kakela site was being watched during the day by a Hui employee, but she'd be an hour or so late getting to her surveillance shift with the visit to her friends' house for dinner—not likely to be a problem now that the thief knew the property was lighted and alarmed.

Sophie's phone rang on the seat beside her. She picked up after checking the caller ID. "Hello, Dr. Taggart."

"Geez, woman, are you always so formal?"

"Hey there, Brett." Sophie hit the speaker feature and set the phone down in the drink holder. "Maui has a cell phone ban, so I have you on speaker."

"Anyone else in the car?"

"No, why?"

"Because I'm paranoid about being caught telling one of my bad archaeology jokes. Here it goes: if you're an archaeologist, does that mean your life is in ruins?"

"I don't know." Sophie frowned. "I suppose most of it would be spent excavating."

"Never mind." Taggart cleared his throat. "I called with some fairly big news. The Hui has received an offer to buy the site from a private company."

Sophie was still puzzling over his question. "I don't see what's funny about what you said. Archaeologists deal with ruins all the time."

"It's stupid. A dumb joke. Never mind, please let's forget it."

"No. I grew up outside the U.S. A lot of colloquialisms are opaque to me."

"See, that's it. Colloquialisms are *opaque*." Taggart snorted a laugh. "Okay. The phrase "life in ruins" means things are going bad in your life—it's a train wreck. Things are falling apart. You're going to the dogs."

"Going to the dogs?"

"Oh please, please forget it and let's move on. Did you hear my news?"

"About the private offer to buy Kakela? What is the significance?" Sophie navigated a traffic light outside of Kahului and turned onto the Hana Highway. Fields of waving green sugarcane bordered the roads, the late afternoon sun gleaming on their sword like leaves. The expanse of open space gave a sense of a green ocean, rippling with wind and leading the eye up the mauve and taupe expanse of Haleakala volcano, wreathed in clouds.

"How much longer do you have on your security contract? For the Hui?"

"It was for two weeks to begin with. I have eight more days."

"Well, a major Hawaii real estate investment firm has made an offer to buy the Kakela site from the Hui. It's a big deal because the offer is significant, and the board is considering it." Taggart named a figure that made Sophie's eyes widen.

"But what about the cultural significance of the site to the whole community, and the state?" Sophie tapped her fingers on the steering wheel as the rental approached the coast. A wind-whipped expanse of waves and cliffs opened up on her left.

"That's a thing, but the party making the offer has included a proposal to excavate the site to the highest standards and to restore it as part of the offer. They want to create a cultural tourist attraction that earns its keep in entrance fees."

Sophie considered this. "What are the negative aspects?"

"You mean the downside?"

"If you want to put it that way. You like colloquialisms."

"Take to 'em like a pig to mud. Honestly, if this offer is sincere, I can't think of one. Other than the Hui losing control of the site, and it being in private hands. I don't honestly care about that one way or the other, as long as the site is properly excavated and restored...and they use my firm to do the work." Taggart gave a dry chuckle. "I'll keep you posted." He ended the call.

Twenty minutes later, Sophie pulled up at the high wooden gate that enclosed Lei and Stevens's property. She pushed the button on the keypad beside the gate. "Hey there. It's Sophie."

"Sophie! Glad you could make it." Stevens, Lei's husband,

had a mellow baritone voice rendered hollow by the intercom. The gate retracted on its wheeled axis, and Sophie drove forward, up the curving driveway past the orange and lemon trees and Lei's father Wayne's cottage. She drew up and parked in front of the sturdy wooden plantation style home that Lei and Stevens had purchased with Lei's inheritance from a recently deceased aunt.

Her friend met her at the door of the cottage, their son Kiet on one hip. The baby was astonishingly good-looking. Dark green eyes framed by long, thick lashes, a full head of curly black hair, and pale mocha skin marked his mixed heritage. Kiet's striking looks struck a chord in Sophie. Mixed heritage was both beautiful and challenging to live with, as she knew firsthand— but Hawaii was one of the best places in the United States in which to be a person of color. She was just another drop in the sea of races that made their home in the Islands.

Kiet reached dimpled hands toward Sophie, burbling something adorable.

Sophie took the baby in her arms. "He just said 'Auntie Sophie.' Could he be any more beautiful?"

Lei laughed. "Don't really think so. He's an exceptionally cute baby, and he knows it."

Stevens pushed the front door wide, coming out to join them on the front porch. "Aren't you a sight for sore eyes! Your face looks wonderful, Sophie. So good to see you and glad you're okay."

Sophie felt the quick sting of tears as the tall, rangy, blue-eyed man she had come to think of as a brother embraced her, along with the baby.

"Thanks. It's nice of you to say so, but that scar…"

"Just adds character," Stevens said. "If anything, you look a little dangerous. And sexy." He wiggled his brows.

Lei punched him in the arm. "Hey, I'm right here!"

Stevens winced theatrically. "Like you would let me forget it."

Bickering playfully, the two went into the house. Sophie followed more slowly, the baby on her hip, pausing to greet Keiki, Lei's well-mannered Rottweiler, leaning Kiet down so he could tug on the dignified dog's ears, babbling the while.

Looking around the humble, well-worn living room, Sophie felt a painful tightness in her chest.

This.

This was something she wanted.

*A home. A child. A man to joke with, laugh with, and kiss…*as Lei and Stevens were doing in the kitchen, their passion for each other seemingly undiluted by marriage and parenthood.

Dinner was casual and noisy as Jared, Stevens's firefighter brother, a recent transplant from California, joined them at the picnic table in the dining room along with Lei's father, Wayne. Shoyu chicken, rice, a big salad, and Antigua's pupu were enhanced by beer, and provided a simple and delicious meal. Sophie took it all in, even exchanging flirtatious comments with Jared.

Jared was just as physically riveting as his brother. Short dark hair set off a face more handsome than Stevens's rugged one, but his blue eyes were the same crystal color. He had asked Sophie out in the past, and she had refused on the grounds that along-distance relationship was too difficult to maintain—but there was no denying the man's attractiveness. A firefighter who enjoyed ocean sports, Jared was obviously enjoying life on Maui as he told stories of his various adventures.

Wayne doted on the baby and fed him in his highchair. Wayne's silver-shot, curly black hair, craggy features, and many tattoos gave him a rakish look at odds with the tender manner in which he cared for the child. Watching that made Sophie miss her father, Frank Smithson. The most nurturing person in her life, her ambassador father traveled a lot, but when he was home, he'd always lavished her with his full attention, as if to make up for her mother's emotional absence.

Pim Wat Smithson's chronic depression had kept her from being much more than a nominal parent. Sophie's nannies had tried, but no one had filled the longing in her heart to be close to her mother, a longing that had led to her agreement to a disastrous early arranged marriage to much older businessman Assan Ang—a relationship that had nearly cost her life.

Jared touched her arm. "You keep making googly eyes at that baby, and I'll start to think you're in the market for one."

Sophie smiled. "I would not be averse, were the situation to be right."

"You sure you want to keep turning me down, then?" The teasing light in Jared's eyes made Sophie laugh. "I'm not averse, either."

"Sorry. I'm dating someone." Sophie felt a blush heat her neck. Marcella would know how to turn his jokes back on him, but Sophie just verbally stumbled and stuttered.

"Oh, ho! Who is the lucky gentleman?" Stevens asked.

"Someone I work with on Oahu." Sophie found herself reluctant to talk or joke about Connor—the relationship was so new and so complex that it wasn't the sort of thing she wanted bandied about. Lei gave her a wink as she fetched the baby's sippy cup.

The evening passed pleasantly, and all too soon she was saying her goodbyes. Out on the porch she embraced her friend. "I'm so happy for you and your family. I hope I have something half as happy as you do, someday."

"You will." Lei cupped Sophie's damaged cheek gently. "It

really is healing well." The touch felt good on Sophie's numb-but-tingly skin. She wondered when the graft would stop feeling so strange—the doctor had said it could take months for the nerves to begin to fire correctly.

"I'm so glad you came," Lei said. "I never expected this to be my life, either, and I'm grateful. I hope I see a lot more of you while you're here on Maui."

* * *

Sophie had wrapped up the evening early with Lei and her family in order to get back to the Kakela site, but it was fully dark when she arrived. The grounds appeared secure as Sophie trudged to the trailer, fighting the familiar black fog of depression. She hung her backpack on the wall inside the door.

The contrast of her current life with Lei's rich one could not have been greater.

Moving on autopilot, she went through her work shift start routine: booting up the surveillance equipment, checking the monitors, and a walk around the grounds to make sure everything was secure and undisturbed.

She mulled over the evening's social events as she walked around the deserted site. Warm wind, scented with mangoes and plumeria, teased her nostrils as she swung the heavy flashlight back and forth, not really needed as the sensor lights burst on with her movement. Nothing appeared to be out of place until she reached the corner where the dig areas were covered with plywood.

One of the pieces of plywood was out of alignment. Likely someone from the Hui had moved it to show someone the dig area.

As Sophie tugged the wood back into place, she spotted a flash of color inside the deep, straight-sided rectangular excavation that Taggart had called a "test unit." She pushed the plywood back, shone her flashlight into the pit, and gasped.

Chapter 6

A man's body lay in the bottom of the perfectly rectangular hole, curled on its side. The means of death was clearly visible: the back of the man's head was virtually gone where it had been bashed in.

Sophie squatted and shone her light over the body, taking in the details. He wore an Aloha shirt and chinos, Hawaii business casual, and a pair of tan boat shoes. The victim's complexion was the olive-brown of mixed Hawaiian race. Height seemed around five foot ten, sturdy build. His black hair had silver at the temples—not that much was visible with the amount of blood that stained it.

She played the light over his face again: she'd only met the man once, but she was pretty sure this was Seth Mano, president of the Hui to Restore Kakela's board.

Sophie slid her cell phone out of her pocket and called her friend. "Lei, we have a big problem here at Kakela."

* * *

Sophie stood back from the crime scene, her arms folded on her chest, as Lei climbed down into the hole with The University of Hawaii crime scene intern she was working with at Kahului station.

Once again, as she watched the team, she wondered about her decision to leave the FBI. It was almost painful to be sidelined from her own case just as it escalated in stakes and importance.

"Sophie!" Lei's voice summoned her to the edge of the pit. It was five feet down, so the top of Lei's curly head was just above the edge. "Did you look for the original crime scene on the grounds?"

"No. It occurred to me that he might've been killed here, but I called you first, then 911. I stayed by the body so as not to disturb any possible evidence more than I already had."

"Good." Lei turned to the two officers who had arrived in response to Sophie's call. "Do a sweep of the grounds and look for any signs of disturbance."

"I made it halfway around the left side of the enclosure," Sophie told the officers. That part is clear." The two nodded and set off, their flashlights swinging, even though Sophie had turned on all the lights and the field was lit up as if for a game.

"Glad Captain Omura was okay with giving me the case since I was already familiar with the surveillance going on out here. How did this body get in here when you had monitoring set up for the site? Don't you have cameras on it?" Lei didn't sound accusing, just puzzled as she studied the body.

"The Hui has a staffer keep an eye on the site during the day while I sleep and they don't use the monitors in broad daylight. I turn the cameras on when I come in." Sophie's belly tightened at the conversations she knew were ahead about her surveillance plan, which, in hindsight, had holes in it. "I knew there would be about an hour between when that person, a clerk named Fran, went home and when I came on, since I was having dinner at your house." Sophie found herself rubbing the skin graft on her face and put her hand in her pocket. "I am so upset that I didn't take this more seriously, but we were guarding against theft, not murder!"

Pono Kaihale, Lei's long-time Hawaiian partner, strode across the grass toward them. He folded muscular arms across his barrel chest as he reached the area. "Of course you girls found a body," he said, brown eyes creased in brackets of good humor. "You couldn't just do pedicures like normal ladies."

"You're married to Tiare," Lei said from inside the pit, speaking of Pono's highly industrious and competent wife. "You of all people should understand that work comes first. Get your lazy butt down here and help me check this out."

"Looks muddy. I can see just fine from here." Pono squatted to look down at the body. "What have we got?"

Sophie recapped the little that she knew. "I think it's a man I met recently. Seth Mano."

Lei put a gloved hand into the man's pocket and removed a wallet. She flipped it open. "Yep. Seth Mano. Five foot eleven, one ninety, black hair, brown eyes, aged forty-seven. No cash here."

"Dr. Gregory is on his way." Pono said.

Lei patted the man's pockets, pulling out an empty money clip. "Could be a robbery gone bad." She held her flashlight up to shine upon his wrist, where a tan line showed. "Did he wear an expensive watch?"

"I think so." Sophie remembered something gleaming and heavy on the man's wrist. "He's the head of the Hui's board of directors."

Both Lei and Pono's sharp dark eyes pinned her. "You were telling me there were issues," Lei said. "Apparently, they came to a head." She shook her head, looking down at the man's body. "Bad pun, sorry. So, this is no simple mugging gone wrong with a convenient body dump. At first glance, it looks to me like someone was angry with this person and sending a message."

Pomai Magnuson's set face as she glared at Mano in their last meeting came to mind. But no…Pomai seemed like such a nice woman. She wouldn't do such a thing. *Would she?* But Sophie had learned that most people had the capacity to kill when the motivation was right. "I'll have to tell you two everything I know about what's going on at the Hui," Sophie said. "I am so new on the job here, though. Brett Taggart is the one who will know more, and all the players involved."

Pono was already jotting the name on a spiral notebook.

"Detectives!" The voice of one of the officers snapped all three of their heads around. "Come see this!"

Pono gave Lei a hand up out of the pit as she ascended the ladder, and the three of them hurried across the field to an area just outside the front gate.

The two officers shone their lights on a scuffed area of dirt near the gate. Sophie must've walked right past it when she entered less than an hour before. One of the officers held his light on a smooth, round black stone fetched up against the chain-link fence. The rock was roughly the size of a pineapple and was one of many used to construct a low stone platform that marked the entrance to the site.

"Looks like it could be the murder weapon," Lei said, shining a light on the rusty bloodstain on the stone. "Tape this area, will you?"

Pono took out his recorder. "Sophie, mind if I get an official statement from you in the trailer?"

Just then the medical examiner's van pulled up. Portly Dr. Gregory, in an Aloha shirt decorated with rainbows, and his assistant Dr. Tanaka, pulled their gurney out of the back. Lei went to speak to them as the officers cordoned off the crime scene.

"Of course I'll give you a statement." Sophie led Pono to the trailer, battling a sense of displacement and a nagging jealousy.

This was her job. Her crime scene. And now she was just a bit player in whatever came next. She was tired of being jealous of her friend Lei. She needed to get over that, and fast.

She gave Pono her statement and everything she could think of about the Hui and its inner workings, and he eventually flipped his notebook shut and turned off the recorder. "I better get out there. You can…" He looked around at the barren setting, the monitors filled with activity as the investigation progressed and more MPD staff arrived. "I guess you can watch from here."

"I'll stay here in case you need me," Sophie said stiffly. "I have some phone calls to make to inform Security Solutions and the Hui."

"Don't give any details," Pono said. "In fact, hold off on any of those calls except to Security Solutions. We need to control all communications and observe reactions to the murder."

Sophie tightened her lips. "Of course."

Pono pushed out the door, letting it shut with a bang and leaving her to watch the investigation on the monitors.

"I have an incident on the job to report," Sophie said to Kendall Bix, Vice President of operations and her immediate supervisor, when she reached him on the satellite phone Security Solutions had issued her. She repeated the information about the body discovery.

"So how long was the site unmonitored between when the Hui's watchman left and you came on duty?" Bix was sharp enough to catch on to that and ask that question—he was always paying attention to the bottom line, and how it would affect their company.

"About an hour." Sophie pinched the bridge of her nose, closing her eyes. "This was not my fault."

"I never said it was. I just asked you how long the site was empty and unmonitored, providing a window for murder."

"I had dinner with friends. I thought things were covered enough considering the level of threat, which was burglary. Not violence." Sophie's stomach churned and she wished she hadn't eaten so much shoyu chicken.

"And the surveillance monitors you installed?"

"They were off when I arrived. They do not use them during the day, and they had not turned them on prior to my arrival."

"Who's the day personnel?"

"A woman staffer associated with the Hui. I just told them to hire someone during the day, or keep it covered with existing staff..."

"This is bad." Bix's voice was uncompromising. "You were in charge of security. You should have vetted any staff having anything to do with the monitoring of the site. You should have known and trained anyone covering the site on the equipment and established a protocol so that the site was never unmonitored, no matter the threat level."

Sophie swallowed. "I can see that now. I am not used to...that is, I have never devised and covered a job like this before. Clearly, I allowed a window of opportunity for someone to take advantage."

"We will discuss this thoroughly on your return. I'd be surprised if you aren't fired immediately. I'd fire you, if I were the Hui, and I might still fire you when you get back." Bix hung up his phone.

Familiar depression rose around her. Sophie wanted to curl up in a ball under her desk.

But if she did, she might never come back out, and Lei and

Pono might still need her help—so instead she dropped to the dirty floor and began pushups. Took out her exercise ball and sat down on it and began sit-ups.

She was still doing those when Lei poked her head into the trailer. Lei's curly hair was escaping her ponytail in a backlit nimbus and her tilted eyes were bright with the excitement of the hunt. "You can go back to your condo, Sophie. We're going to search this and the entire grounds with a fine-toothed comb for any evidence and line up interviews with all the names you gave us, starting with Magnuson and Taggart. I'll let you know if there's anything more we need from you, but you might as well get some rest. At least one of us can."

Sophie's body felt like lead as she stood and stowed the exercise equipment. "I just feel sick that this happened on my watch. Literally."

Lei shrugged. "Murder doesn't play favorites. Yeah, you could have had a tighter eye on things here, but it just would have meant his body turned up somewhere else most likely—and from my perspective, the body dump being here is convenient. The window between the daytime watch and your return gives us a narrow time frame for the murder, which is good in terms of catching the doer. But I'm not having to answer to a boss about it." Lei smiled, and patted Sophie's shoulder. "You can always go back to the FBI if Security Solutions fires you."

"Ha," Sophie said humorlessly, preceding her friend across the brightly lit field to the gate. That wasn't going to happen. Ever. "More likely I'll apply with Honolulu Police Department. Don't worry about me and my job. Catch this killer—and let me help you, any way I can."

"Will do." But the sound of the gate clanging shut sounded very final as Lei closed Sophie out of the site.

Chapter 7

The condo, with its peeling whale decals and smell of plastic cleaner, oppressed Sophie the minute she came in. It was still early, only eight p.m., and sleep was out of the question. Sophie tossed her backpack onto the couch and opened the slider. Warm, damp night air smelling of the ocean washed over her. She walked out onto the little balcony and leaned on the metal railing, looking out over Ma`alea Harbor.

Stars pierced a black velvet sky, and palms framing the building floors below shushed in the wind off the sea. The moon wasn't visible yet, but it would come out by one a.m., as she had reason to know from her graveyard shift at the Kakela site.

If only she knew Maui better, enough to find somewhere to run late at night. There was a beach nearby, but the talons of depression had already begun to clamp down on her brain.

There were too many triggers: Lei's home and family. Making a mistake that had opened Kakela up to become a crime site. Being sidelined and displaced from what should be her case—but wasn't.

Somehow, that it was her friend Lei displacing her increased the sting. She wondered when she would be done second-guessing her choice to move to the private sector.

Sophie missed Connor with a sudden ache, and reached for her phone—but then, she'd have to talk to him like he was her boss, report the problem, endure his reaction to her oversight with Kakela's security…and she just didn't have the wherewithal to deal with it right now.

She set the phone back down.

Only her computer world could comfort her right now and head off the depression. That, and some yoga.

She booted up her laptop and took a quick shower, washing the sweat of the crime scene and stress away.

If only she could wash away her discouragement so easily…

Sophie towel-dried, and then spread the big, thick beach towel provided for guests on the floor. Still nude, as she liked to be in private, she did several sun salutations facing the black expanse of the unseeing ocean, and finally sat cross-legged, with her laptop open on the coffee table.

Maybe DAVID could find something that would help the investigation. The rogue program's ability to penetrate and mine law enforcement databases for information using keywords was totally unsanctioned, and the fight for possession had ultimately tipped her into leaving the FBI. Ever since she left the Bureau and went to work at Security Solutions, she had avoided using the program with its unresolved privacy and consent issues, but tonight she felt the frustration driving her back to that comfort zone.

She plugged in her Bose headphones and pulled up the program's search window as her favorite Beethoven sonata filled her ears…and that made her think of Connor again.

Connor played violin like she worked computers: instinctively, with a loss of self, and a perfectionism honed by intense self-discipline. He'd finally played for her, this very song—and missed a note somewhere along the way.

He'd begun again, and she'd enjoyed it just as much the

second time: the afternoon light from the window falling over his tilted head; those muscular arms holding the delicate instrument like the hollow, fragile wooden shell it was, while attacking it with passion—coaxing an incredible range of sound from it that reminded Sophie of a human voice singing.

She'd had a music appreciation class at her finishing school in Geneva, and had always been drawn to classical as the proper background music for her computer work—but never had she been so close to this level of skill and focus, and it was unbearably arousing.

She'd kissed him after, rising from the couch where she was sitting and hooking an arm around his neck, drawing him down to meet her mouth…*and it had been so good.*

Connor was the one to slow things down, setting aside the violin and touching her lips with his thumb. "Not yet. I want to date you first. Let's go slow. Anticipation is the spice of life." He was so disciplined about everything he did—and he was right. But so far, they'd only had one date, and she felt more than ready for more.

These recollections were not helping her get anything done but feel more depressed and sexually frustrated as she sat in this awful condo alone, unable to contact him without dealing with the shitstorm she was caught in.

Sophie refocused on the search keyword box that popped up on DAVID's opening screen. She typed in Seth Mano's name and began a search for his background. While DAVID sifted through the cyber sphere for information, she opened up one of her old caches.

She hadn't checked on the Ghost's activities since she had left her father's apartment the first time—the truth was, she hadn't wanted to know. Now she couldn't resist looking, like picking at a scab.

Her eyes widened and her body stiffened as she read.

The cache was full of mysterious situations in which the Ghost's invisible vigilante influence was readily discernible: bank robbers who turned their guns on each other. The CEO of a petrochemical corporation who called in to blow the whistle on his own company. Stock traders who turned in those giving them illegal tips. Dirty cops caught returning money they'd skimmed off of drug busts to the evidence room.

Gang leaders meeting to parley, and shooting each other instead.

That was one of the Ghost's favorite moves: hacking the cell phones of crime lords and sending them texts that turned them against each other. It was almost a signature move.

"They have their uses, and they have expiration dates when those uses are done," he'd told her when she confronted him.

Sophie swallowed at the crime scene photos of that case.

He had never even slowed down his vigilante activities through the whole eight months they had been aware of each other. According to DAVID's collection, he was pulling off a vigilante coup of some kind at least weekly.

Sophie slammed the lid of the laptop down. Her breath heaved through her lungs as if she'd been running.

She had told him how she felt about his activities: that she couldn't support it or agree with it; that she couldn't believe it was right for one man to be judge and jury.

"You're a hypocrite, *Mary Watson*," he'd said, referring to the identity she used when she went off the grid.

And in the end, she'd admitted that she *was* a hypocrite, that she understood the utility of what he did in reaching criminals that the law never would, and she'd even had him extract her sadistic ex's child bride from her gilded cage.

They'd left it that they would agree to disagree on the

issue...*but somehow she'd believed he heard her, that he was changing, that he understood and respected her enough to listen to her on something so important.*

Tears of anger and disappointment pricked her eyes. *"Demon spawn of the accursed,"* Sophie swore in Thai.

Her phone dinged with a text message, and her eyes widened when she saw it was from Connor. The timing was awfully coincidental.

She wouldn't put it past Connor to be spying on her through her laptop—certainly he had the skills to do that...*but he wouldn't, would he?* He had before, but that was back when they were adversaries.

Rage filled Sophie at the thought of her laptop's camera eye being used to watch as Sophie sat naked in front of it...and of course, the Ghost would have cloned her machine and would be observing what she was doing on DAVID, and online.

He'd have confirmation that she knew that he was still up to his vigilantism.

She clicked on the text message.

Every chiseled muscle was poetic in its clarity in the black-and-white composition of a photo of Connor playing violin, naked from the waist up. Anubis, his Doberman, gazed at his master with devoted focus, the dog's head even with Connor's waist.

The picture was good enough to blow up and frame on the wall—excellent, like everything he did. Sexy and refined, artistic, a carefully chosen bit of theater for her appreciation— one that he knew would get to her.

It was like Connor was reading her mind—*but he was probably just spying on her!*

Another text message arrived from him with an innocuous *ding.*

Was thinking of you as I played this piece.

Sophie stood up and stalked back and forth to discharge her anger, gathering her thoughts and deciding how to respond.

She picked up her phone and stabbed out a message with her thumbs. *Quit spying on me or you'll see things you don't want to see, just like I did when I logged into DAVID and saw what you've been up to. Clearly my feelings and convictions don't mean anything to you, so I don't know where that leaves us.*

Sophie set the phone down again, and stomped into the bedroom to change. She came out dressed in the short black Lycra dress with the flirty skirt she'd brought for social occasions. By all that was unholy, her alter ego Mary Watson was going out.

Sophie was done waiting, waiting, waiting…to be healed and not so afraid, then to be in love, then for the right moment, the right mood, *the right man.*

Maybe there was no right man for her, and she'd always be alone.

But she didn't have to be celibate. It was time to get over the issues left over from her violent marriage, and just 'get laid' as the Americans called it.

Sophie slid her feet into the sensible strappy black sandals she'd brought, grabbed her square wallet and keys, and headed for the door, turning off the already-vibrating phone.

She was going to Lahaina to find a bar.

And she wasn't planning to come back to the condo alone.

Chapter 8

Sophie had adopted the identity of Mary Watson months ago when she went off the grid the first time. Mary Watson knew how to handle men, wasn't afraid of being attractive, and didn't have issues in the bedroom. The feminine, fun-loving identity was a way that Sophie could leave her past behind. And, sitting at the bar looking over the glitter of light on the water of Lahaina Bay, Sophie decided that putting on Mary Watson was like donning a party dress—just what she needed.

She stirred a pale blue drink shaded by a small paper umbrella, and smiled at the man who had taken the seat beside her.

"I would offer to buy you a drink, but I can see that you already have one," he gestured to his own pale green concoction in a martini glass. "Do you think less of me for liking appletinis?"

Mary Watson laughed, and smoothed her short skirt. "I like someone who's secure enough to buy whatever kind of drink he likes. My name's Mary."

"I'm Chad." A shirt in faded chambray draped the man's muscular shoulders, and the hands holding the martini glass were rough with calluses. One of his thumbnails was dark with a blood blister—he'd probably hit it with a hammer.

She pointed. "I see you are in the construction trade."

Chad's brown eyes widened, and he grinned. "You a detective?" His smile was not unattractive, a pleasing composition of simple enjoyment and anticipation.

"Sometimes. In another life." She lifted her drink and tipped it toward him. "To new identities." *He would do for what she had in mind.*

"Is this seat taken?"

Sophie turned her head to see the new arrival. Brett Taggart took off that Indiana Jones hat and set it on the bar. "Never know when a bad day will start looking up."

Sophie leaned forward and drew a deep draft of the sweet, foamy drink through her straw as her stomach plummeted. *She might not be getting laid after all.* "They say it's a small island. I guess it's true. Hello, Dr. Taggart. *Brett.*" Sophie said his first name as he raised a brow at her. She stirred the dregs of her drink and lifted a finger for the bartender. "Give me a cosmopolitan this time."

The man with the appletini got up and left with a little headshake.

"I'd like it if this was the Old West and they just parked a bottle of whiskey next to my elbow," Taggart said. "It's been that kind of day."

"I take it you heard about the body." Sophie watched the bartender shake her drink.

"Just got done being interviewed by MPD. Not fun." Taggart threw back the whiskey shot he'd ordered, and tapped the bar for another.

"Guess we are both out of a job for a while." Sophie accepted her new drink and sipped it. She hardly ever imbibed, and the first one was already having an effect.

"Yeah. Won't be doing much at the site with it being a crime scene." Taggart threw back his second shot and tapped for a third.

"You appear to take your drinking seriously. No frills."

"I'm a purist. When I do something, I do it one hundred percent and with total focus." Taggart was wearing a tight black tee and worn jeans that made her want to touch them. He narrowed piercing dark eyes at her. "And I'm good with my hands."

Sophie felt a tingle.

The guy with the appletini had not given her a tingle.

Sophie lifted her glass. "To drowning our sorrows, as they say in America—with total focus." They touched rims, and the chime of the glasses reverberated through her. "What did you tell the investigators?"

"Can we not talk about that?"

"Don't know what else we have in common." The second drink went off like a bomb in her empty stomach, and heat flowed out from that empty place inside her, running along her nerve endings and relaxing her stiff spine into a supple curve.

"We have this. Being alone in a bar, getting drunk." Taggart picked up his third drink.

Sophie turned her head to him, and smiled. "Not alone anymore."

Taggart's grin was much better than the man's with the appletini—it framed straight white teeth and lifted his cheeks into well-worn creases that bracketed his eyes with intelligence and humor. "You are so right."

He leaned over, sliding a hand around the back of her neck, and drew Sophie toward him.

His kiss was assertive, confident, and thorough. Sophie liked the taste of whiskey on his tongue, the smell of tobacco, with all its associations, in the warm place beside his ear.

He let her go eventually. They both sat back. Sophie finished her drink and lifted a finger for another. "That was nice."

"I knew it would be." Taggart sipped his whiskey this time. "I wanted to do that from the minute I met you."

"Oh." Sophie kept her eyes forward, trying to figure out what she was feeling.

Meeting him here was ideal in some ways. She was sure Taggart knew what he was doing in the bedroom, and she felt safe with him, which was no small thing. Plus, he lived here, and there was little likelihood of a messy entanglement with her home on another island.

But they were working together, and there had just been a murder on their mutual job site, and she was pretty sure that tomorrow, in the cold hard light of day, it wouldn't seem like a good idea after all.

It sure seemed like one now.

Taggart picked up her hand. He stroked her fingers, and it sent ripples of sensation through her arms, tightening her nipples. "You have beautiful hands."

Connor had done the same thing to her hand, and *Connor loved her.* Connor was waiting for her to be ready. He was wooing her, respecting her, and trying, in his way, to be honest. She didn't really believe he would spy on her—he had his own code of ethics. Yes, the timing was surprising, but not really. They were both alone in the evening. That's usually when they texted.

He had never told her he had stopped being the Ghost, just because she wished he had.

Sophie gently removed her hand. "I don't think this is going to happen."

"It's such a bad idea that it's good." Taggart leaned over and kissed her again, but this time it felt invasive, taking too much.

She pulled back. "I think you should leave. We've both had a lot to drink."

"You're probably right. Good thing I live nearby and don't have to drive." He lifted his brows. "Sure you won't change your mind, come see the back alleys of Lahaina?"

"No. Thanks."

"Well, too bad." Taggart showed no effect from the shots he'd consumed. He pushed a hand through his hair and clapped the hat back on. "Thanks for making a terrible day just a little bit better." Taggart threw a couple of twenties on the bar. "Another time, perhaps."

Sophie waited until he was gone before she finished her drink and slid off the stool. Her wobbly legs eventually took her outside of the bar, and she breathed drafts of fresh air, hoping the nausea and whirlies would go away. *She probably should have eaten something during her drinking binge.* There was no way she could drive back to Ma'alea.

But there was someone she could call. Someone who would drop everything and come rescue her, no questions asked, whenever she needed it.

Even with her eyes crossing, Sophie knew the number to press on the favorites list of her phone. "I'm sorry, but I think I need a ride."

* * *

Sophie had resumed her spot at the bar and had consumed two more drinks, along with a plate of nachos, by the time Jake Dunn arrived, striding through the crowded bar. He elbowed the man next to her aside with a glare.

"What brought this on?" Jake slid her off the stool and hooked her arm around his neck as her knees buckled.

She fumbled for her purse. "I have to pay."

"Hey. The lady and I were having a conversation…" The man beside her was foolish enough to object, but shut his mouth at one glance from Jake's steely gray eyes.

Sophie giggled. "You're scary, Jake. But not to me." She put a handful of bills on the counter and Jake supported her out.

"You're giggling. How weird," he said, and she giggled some more. He was big as a house and warm as a stove. Leaning on him felt as natural as if she'd been doing it her whole life.

Once in his rental car, a shiny black Ford Escape, Sophie leaned her head back against the seat. "I found a body at the site. I'm in big trouble for letting a murder happen there."

"I heard. Bix called me." Jake reached across her and pulled her seatbelt down and buckled it. His big shoulder was nearby, and she leaned her head on it. Her breast brushed his arm, and it felt good.

"You're drunk." He pushed her upright and reached over to recline her seat, so abruptly that she fell back and away.

"I know."

Jake turned on the SUV with a roar and pulled out.

Sophie turned her head to look at him. It was clear that Jake wanted her, and had since they first met. Why had she resisted the obvious until now? "Take me to bed. I want to have sex."

A long silence.

"Was that rude? I am sometimes socially awkward, I know. But I am just saying what we're both thinking about."

Jake had his eyes on the road and both hands on the wheel, and he was way too far away with his warm, hard muscles. Sophie burped delicately. "Did you hear me? I just propositioned you." She put her hand on his leg. "You're really very attractive, Jake. I'm sorry I never told you that before, but I didn't want to make your big head bigger. So, let's do it."

"This isn't how I want this to go." Jake tightened his big hands on the steering wheel. "No. It's not going to happen this way."

"Don't be so mean. I know you want to." The whirlies got worse, and Sophie swallowed some nausea. *Maybe the nachos hadn't been a good thing after all.*

"I'm not going to be your drunken hookup. It's going to be a hell of a lot more, or nothing."

"Didn't know you were so…" Sophie couldn't think of the word, but suddenly knew she was in trouble. "Pull over! I'm going to be sick."

And she was. She puked into the grass on the side of the Pali Highway, lit up by the headlights of passing cars, with Jake Dunn keeping her from falling over.

Chapter 9

"*Spawn of a worm-riddled water buffalo,*" Sophie cursed, holding her head in both hands as she put her feet on the floor for the first time the next day. "Oh. My. Oh. This hurts."

Piercing sunlight struck her aching eyes like a blow. She'd blocked it out by hanging extra blankets over the windows on previous nights, but hadn't been in any shape to do so last night. Cramps knotted her abused belly. Her head was a huge, throbbing drum. "So this is a hangover."

Her first hangover ever reminded her of Dante's *Inferno*. The sheer physical misery wasn't something she wanted to repeat, but it included memories that made her groan afresh: propositioning Jake; throwing up on the side of the road; Jake carrying her in and putting her to bed…

Sophie was still wearing her dress, but her shoes were set neatly side-by-side near the closet. She spotted a bottle of water and pile of analgesics on her nightstand, along with a note written on the back of a receipt.

She crawled up the bed to the nightstand, unscrewed the water bottle, swallowed four of the pills and drained the bottle.

Hangovers were caused by dehydration. Who knew that

could lead to so many terrible symptoms? Or that drunkenness caused such embarrassing behavior? Certainly she'd heard stories from Marcella, even seen a few examples…but the reality was way worse than she'd ever imagined.

She groaned aloud again, remembering how Jake had rejected her, and had held her up while she vomited. *"Oh, son of a three-headed toad…"*

Sophie picked up the receipt and made her eyes focus. Jake's handwriting was a mass of blocky hieroglyphics, slashes and dots that almost broke the paper's surface. *"Drink lots of water. Get some rest. Someday we will laugh about this."*

Not likely.

She'd never laugh about Jake saying, *"I'm not going to be your drunken hookup. It's going to be a hell of a lot more, or nothing."*

Memory was fuzzy after that, but that sentence was glaringly clear, and made her squirm.

Self-hatred rolled over her in a greasy black wave, along with nausea, and she barely made it to the bathroom in time to lose the bottle of water and painkillers into the toilet.

She staggered back into the bedroom and hung the blankets over the brightly glaring windows to shut out the light.

Hours later, she was finally upright and had a shower, but the depression had replaced the hangover. She went back to bed with a handful of rice crackers and another bottle of water and more aspirin, and fell asleep.

Late in the afternoon, she felt strong enough to retrieve her phone and check her messages. Connor's number showed several calls but he had not left messages. *Typical.* He would not want to leave any sort of recording, especially about That Subject, but finally, there was a short one in his fake Aussie accent. "Miss you. Call me. We need to talk."

"Talking won't change anything," Sophie said aloud, and deleted the message. She didn't see him giving up being a vigilante unless he was locked up, or dead. Neither of those options appealed, and her belly cramped at the thought. She plugged her phone back in and lay down, letting the depression suck her down and under like quicksand. She flashed to her mother, lying in bed—her wide, dark eyes fixed on the ceiling, her skin sallow and glossy black hair lank, her lips moving but forming no sound.

Sophie's depression wasn't that bad. *She would never let it get that bad.* She had her father Frank Smithson's big, strong, powerful energy to combat the psychological weakness she'd inherited from her mother, Pim Wat.

She nibbled another cracker as the next message came on.

"Sophie, it's Lei. We are making some progress on the case and wanted to give you an update and get your help on a few things. Call me."

And finally, Jake.

"Hey, partner." An uneasy throat-clearing. "Hope you don't remember too much of what went on last night. But if you do— don't stress about it. Drunk talk is crazy; you wouldn't want to hear some of the things I've done in my time. So just put it behind you, drink your water, and we'll both forget it ever happened, okay? Okay. See you soon. We should discuss the situation at Kakela when you're feeling better."

"Thank you, Jake." Sophie breathed. Thank God he had left that message, or her best solution would be to avoid and try not to see him. *Ever again.*

Sophie drank the rest of the remaining bottle of water, and called Lei.

"Hi, Sophie." Lei's voice sounded annoyingly loud, and Sophie lowered the volume on her phone, wincing.

"Hello, Lei. What's new on the case?" Sophie tried to sound sharp and on top of things.

"You sick? You sound like you've been licking a bad stretch of road," Lei said. *So much for on top of things.*

"I went out and got drunk. Not an experience I care to repeat," Sophie rubbed the tingly-numb skin graft on her face.

"Oh no. I hope it wasn't because of the case! Because I need you, it turns out."

"Well, it was a little bit. I still have to talk to Magnuson, but I expect to be fired."

"No, no. I already took care of it." Lei cut her off. "I spoke to Pomai this morning and told her I thought you'd done a fine job considering no one expected more than someone to come into the site and dig a few more holes. I asked if you could help me with the artifacts burglary aspect of the case for the remaining time on your contract, and she agreed."

"Thanks, Lei." Sophie swallowed a lump in her throat. "That's very kind. You and I both know I screwed up, and it won't be the last time."

"I've done way worse and still ended solving the cases. So, don't beat yourself up. Get in the shower, drag on some clothes, and meet with me and Pono at the Kahului station. We're setting up a murder board, and would like your thoughts."

"On my way." Sophie ended the call, swung her legs off the bed, sat up, and stopped abruptly to keep her brain from sloshing.

She was going to have to move a little more slowly, to begin with.

* * *

Sophie entered the square, putty-colored, urban-ugly Kahului Police Department headquarters an hour later, her head relatively high and step cautiously stable. The headache still pounded at the backs of her eyes, but felt manageable, and she was glad of this distraction to lift her self-esteem. Lei met Sophie in the lobby once she'd texted her arrival.

"Hey." Lei grinned. "The walking dead arrives." Lei's curly hair was escaping its ponytail, and a pair of black jeans and a red tank top with a buff-colored cotton jacket hiding her shoulder holster completed her friend's usual detective outfit. "How's the hangover?"

"Not something I want to repeat."

Lei laughed. "Follow me. I promise Pono and I will keep the lights low to accommodate your handicapped state."

Sophie followed her friend down a hallway past the intake desk and through a beehive of modular units and down another hall. "I behaved badly when I was drunk."

Lei paused in the hallway. "We're alone here. How badly?" Her brows rose and a dimple appeared in her cheek. "Badly...like, involving men? Because it's about time."

"Yes." Sophie shook her head. "The best thing about it is that nothing actually happened."

"Nothing seems to have been happening with you for a very long time, my friend," Lei said. "You and Remarkian should just hop in bed it and get it over with."

"Maybe." Sophie followed her friend's abrupt push into a nearby conference room, unable to speak of the problems that had come up with Connor. "I'm not sure he's the man for me."

"What?" Lei exclaimed. "He's the perfect guy for you!"

Pono, his broad muscular back turned, spun to face them, capping the dry erase marker he'd been using to make a timeline on the whiteboard. "What man? Sophie's dating? This is a newsflash for all my buddies who've been dreaming from afar."

Sophie narrowed her eyes. "I don't want to talk about it. Tell me what's going on with the case."

"No. This is more interesting, because we're in need of a break." Lei pulled out a chair and dropped into it. "What was this bad behavior you got up to?"

Sophie's face felt so hot her ears were on fire. "I drank too much. Said inappropriate things. Jake had to take me home and...put me to bed."

"Oh my God. *Jake?* Your partner?" Lei clapped her hands to her cheeks as Pono grinned, rubbing his big hands together in anticipation of gossip. Lei and Pono had met Jake on one of their case-related trips to Oahu, and ribbing had ensued ever since. "He's so hot. I don't blame you a bit."

"Oh, and bruddah Jake, he was so shock fo' be used for sex li'dat," Pono slipped into pidgin, grinning. "Give us da scoops, sistah. On a scale of one to ten, how was he?"

"Oh no. No. Nothing happened. He turned me down." Sophie groaned. "Please. The case. Make this stop."

Lei looked at Pono. "Jake turned you down?"

"He has it bad," Pono said to Lei. "Poor buggah."

"I am done talking about this." Sophie folded her arms tightly, and her lips, too. "The case. Or I'm leaving."

Lei sighed. "You're no fun. Okay, we got permission from Pomai Magnuson at the Hui to have you work with us, focusing on the burglary aspect of the case until we've ruled out that it's related to the murder. Right now, we're the only staff assigned to the case and there's a lot to cover, so we need your help." She pushed a pen and paper over to Sophie. "Here's a confidentiality agreement. You can't speak to anyone about the case, not even your immediate supervisor, without our say-so. I have a feeling this one has connections to Oahu, so we want to keep the cone of silence on it as long as possible. That includes Jake, okay?"

"Yes. But you might want to bring him on too."

"We can't afford him." Creases of good humor bracketed Lei's bright brown eyes. "And it appears, you can't either. I'm sure he'd love to help, but for now, you're our girl."

"And I thank you for finding a way for me to be useful." Sophie signed her name to the form.

"You kidding? First thing I want you to do is a deep background on Seth Mano using that off-the-books software you made—DAVID."

Sophie grinned. "Good. Because I already worked up a profile on Mano." She took a stick drive out of her pocket. "I just need a laptop for us to take a look at the information cache. I think you'll be surprised at the president of the board's unsavory connections."

Chapter 10

"No wonder Pomai didn't like this guy," Lei said, as they scrolled through a list of Seth Mano's businesses and connections. "Looks like he had a finger in the Chang crime family endeavors. That art gallery is a front for money laundering. We busted them and shut them down, but six months later they opened another one and were back in business, just hiding it better."

Sophie frowned. "Could the fact that Mano's body was dumped at Kakela be a coincidence? Not related to the looting at the site?"

"Possible. Still possible it's just a robbery gone bad, too. But I don't believe it," Lei said. "I think this has to do with his 'unsavory connections,' as you call it."

"That's what we have you for, Sophie." Pono gave Sophie's shoulder a little punch, and he shook his fingers in exaggerated pain. "Ow. Jealous of your deltoids."

"You have to earn those deltoids, Pono. They don't happen by accident," Sophie said, scrolling further. "What else do you two see in this list? Mano had all the qualifications to be a board member. Did you get to the bottom of the reason for the conflict between him and Pomai Magnuson?"

"Pomai is a friend of my wife's." Pono dropped the jocularity. "And Pomai has grumbled about Mano plenty when at our house. We interviewed her formally yesterday, and she thinks Mano was dirty and had some ulterior motive for his volunteer role as the board president, but she didn't know what it was. She's been trying to figure it out."

"Well, someone had some reason to bash the man's head in," Lei said. "And these crime connections really help us look for motive and people to interview. Can you run a cross-check on people involved with the Hui and his list of roles and connections? Maybe he was meeting someone there and pissed them off."

"So you think it was a...crime of opportunity?"

"Yes, and no." Lei pushed away from the laptop they were perusing and stood up to pace a bit. "We've had longer to speculate on this—since the other night, in fact. We both think the timing of Mano meeting someone at Kakela was no accident. Someone knew when the Hui staffer left for the day, and when you would be returning. We think they arranged for a meeting with Mano—or Mano knew the timing and arranged the meeting—and they took the opportunity to bash his head in and dump him on the grounds, where he wouldn't be discovered for at least some hours—maybe not until the following day."

"They'd be right about that. If the wooden covering over the hole hadn't been moved, I never would have looked inside the excavation site. It might have taken until the next day to notice flies or something," Sophie said. "I appreciate you saying you liked the window of time I left by not covering the surveillance...it didn't help me with my supervisor, but it made me feel a little better about my oversight."

"Honestly, I believe that if you had the site totally covered, they would have had their meet somewhere else. So, who we need to look for is someone associated with the Hui who had some sort of bone to pick with Mano, and got mad enough to kill him—and knew you'd left a window of opportunity for the meet and the body dump."

"I'm pretty sure that's a short list. And Pomai Magnuson's name has to be at the top of it," Sophie said.

"Exactly why we've had her, and Brett Taggart, in for interviews already," Pono said. "And we're having them in for more." He pushed the case jacket file over to Sophie. "You can check out the backgrounds we've run on them, but we'd like to see if you can come up with more with your fancy DAVID program."

"Of course." Sophie pulled the manila case file over and flipped it open. She scanned the brief record checks and driver's license records. "Bare bones here. But at least they don't have any infractions."

"We need the kind of workup that you did on Mano for the remaining board members and the associates we can find attached to Mano," Lei said. "Can I keep this stick drive to print out the information you've got on him?"

"Yes. But you cannot disclose how you got that information, Lei." Sophie held her friend's large, tilted brown eyes with her gaze. "DAVID is mine now, but the program is flagged by the FBI as a possible threat to national security. Which is ridiculous, but the issues around consent they have raised still have to be addressed. I'm not supposed to be using the program."

Lei nodded, reaching out a hand to pull the file back toward her. "I understand. Pono and I discussed bringing you and DAVID on board; we both feel the end justifies the means and you're only giving us background that will help us move forward faster."

"As long as that's the understanding. You can keep the stick drive—but honestly, I'd prefer if you didn't print anything off of it. Go through and look for what you need, then link to the original sources and download it. That way, my butt is covered, too."

Lei cocked her head. "You're getting good at the slang, Sophie. Well, we have a meeting with Dr. Gregory and Mano's body at the morgue tomorrow morning. I'll call you with any results you should know, and any interviews I think you should observe."

"Sounds like a plan." Sophie stood. "I better find my laptop and get on it."

"See, more slang. And sometimes I hardly notice your accent anymore."

Sophie smiled. "You're just getting used to it. But how much better can things get? I love living in Hawaii, and I'm embracing my American side more and more."

"Just don't lose that edge," Pono said. "That edge that makes you good at what you do."

"I don't know how to be any other way," Sophie said. "But you two. You work so well as a team. Jake Dunn and I are still figuring out how to work effectively together. We have such different styles. Was it always that easy between you?"

The two looked at each other and both grinned at the same time. "She my little sistah," Pono said.

"And he my bruddah," Lei replied. "And sometimes we bicker, but it's all in the family. We each have strengths that complement each other's. You guys will figure it out."

Sophie wasn't that sure.

* * *

Sophie was still on her laptop, seated at the coffee table of the condominium, when a knock came at the door.

It had to be Jake. Sophie felt her pulse speed up and her cheeks heat as she mentally composed an apology for her behavior the night before.

Still, she paused to look through the peephole—and saw Connor.

Her heart lurched and squeezed, a sensation like a fist closing tightly around it. She schooled her features into the blank mask that Assan Ang had taught her with his fists, and opened the door. "Connor. What are you doing here?"

Connor's sea-blue eyes were shadowed by an overhead light that fell on his short blond hair and highlighted the musculature of his wide shoulders. He didn't smile. He didn't reach out to her—he just brushed past her and walked in.

"Well. Please, enter." Sophie followed him, anger quickly replacing that first apprehensive surge of excitement she'd felt upon seeing him.

"You weren't answering your phone." Connor's voice was flat, uninflected, the Australian accent that was part of his public persona gone. "I was worried."

Sophie faced him, hands on her hips. "How did you know where I was? Oh, never mind that. You're not only my boss, you're spying on me."

Connor narrowed his eyes. She could see their expression better as the kitchen light fell on his face—a deceptively friendly-looking, handsome face that hid a brilliant and devious mind. "I'm not your boss, and I'm not spying on you. I told you I wouldn't do that."

"You are certainly capable of it, and you seem entirely too well-informed about my activities and location." She'd run a security app on her phone and computer to make sure they were clear of trackers, but still…

"Really?" He threw his hands up in frustration. "Your

location is in the job file! And as to the real problem here, you were the one who was spying on me and got this problem started again!"

Sophie had no response for that, because it was true. "I didn't want to know, before. And then I did."

"And you don't like what you found out, as is often the case. Another good reason I don't spy on you."

They stared at each other, and Sophie felt their breathing fall into sync as a flash of her drinking binge and Jake tucking her into bed filled her mind. *Thank God he wasn't spying on her, or he would know all about that.* She wouldn't put it past him to be able to track her phone and hack the security feed at the bar.

He was even better than her at tech, and there was nothing he couldn't do if he decided to—*it was so damn sexy.*

Sophie tried to resist the attraction. "Do you think coming over here, invading my space, interrupting my work, is a good way to…make friends?"

"I don't want to be your friend. Never did, really. It's always been about more than that, for me at least."

Connor had never held back from telling her how he felt about her, and it was more than slightly terrifying when she was afraid to even know what her own feelings were.

"Too bad, then, when it's clear you don't care about my opinion of your activities." Sophie was getting in touch with the anger that had fueled her withdrawal, her drinking binge, and the impulse to have sex with a stranger.

"I care too much. That's the problem. And I don't know how to do this relationship any more than you do." Connor reached for her, but Sophie stepped back.

"You can begin by listening to me. By respecting what I ask for, and feel." She was surprised by the wave of sadness that replaced the anger as she said those words, and she knew it showed in her eyes. "It hurt to discover that you had not changed or slowed down, even by one iota, the things you were doing."

Sophie couldn't bring herself to say out loud what he was doing. He avoided any mention of his alias in any place that could be overheard by human or electronic ears.

"I thought we agreed to disagree." Sophie saw the same sadness she felt reflected in Connor's eyes. "You didn't ask, and I didn't tell. It seemed the best way to handle things. I'm sorry you feel this way, but it's not something I plan to change."

"Then I don't know where that leaves us, like I told you in my text." Sophie was way too familiar with the ripping, rending sensation of her heart breaking. "It looks like this is over before it ever got going."

Connor's eyes were bleak, the color of clouds over the sea. "You're in charge of where this is going and how fast or slow. If I've put the brakes on a bit, it's because I didn't want you to have any regrets." He blew out a breath. "And unfortunately, our relationship's not the only thing I came to talk to you about."

"What else, then?" Sophie found that she had taken a step closer to him. She wanted to touch him, but wasn't sure how— her inexperience and the chains of her past weighed down her arms. He noticed though, and reached for her, taking her hands in both of his.

"Assan Ang has disappeared."

Sophie was so glad he was holding her hands. His warm palms were the bright point of contact in a universe gone gray and no longer safe—*if it had ever been*. Her ex had sworn to kill her the last time she saw him, and she had no doubt he meant it. "How?" Her lips felt numb, forming the word.

"I have had a contact inside his prison who has kept me

informed. I knew Ang was being extradited to Hong Kong to stand trial. Someone helped him escape en route."

Sophie's knees buckled, and Connor caught her close in a hug that held her up. He was just the right height for her to lean on his shoulder, to feel his arms surround her, creating an illusion of safety.

He was also just the right height for her to feel his heart beating under her cheek, for her to feel his arms closing out the darkness.

"I couldn't tell you that on the phone." Connor's voice was muffled by the thick curling halo of her hair. She felt his lips near her ear, warm and tingling. "I'll keep you safe. I'll find him. And I'll deal with him."

Sophie lifted her head from his shoulder and turned to look at him. Their faces were inches apart as brown eyes clashed with blue. "He's not yours to deal with. *He's mine.* And if you take this from me, we really are finished."

"God, you're sexy," he breathed, and his mouth descended to meet hers.

That conversation they'd been having, the nonverbal conversation about how they would fit together, about how they could be together, about how much they wanted each other and how it would feel—that conversation resumed as if there had been no pause.

No pause to go to another island on a job.

No pause to be disappointed by each other's choices.

No pause to almost sleep with someone else.

Sophie finally broke the kiss, her hands on his chest pushing him gently away. "This doesn't change anything."

"No, it doesn't." Connor slid his hands down her arms, clasped her hands, and squeezed them. "But it might make us both feel a whole lot better about life." He grinned.

Sophie smiled. "I wish I could say yes, invite you in for the night and forget all this. I wish you'd been here yesterday, when that was all I was thinking about doing. But I'm afraid..."

"I know you're afraid, and not just of Ang." Connor squeezed her hands again. "And it's the same reason I am. This is about more than sex. Because if that's all it was..."

"We'd have been doing it like bunnies," Sophie said. "As Marcella would say."

Connor smiled, touched her nose. "Exactly." He walked over to the sliding glass doors. Ocean-scented breeze blew in over them. The soft clatter of that night wind in the coconut trees four floors below made music with the distant rush of waves. The moon, just rising, left silver tracks on the water. "Not a bad view for such a dumpy condo."

Sophie joined him. Looking out across the inky sea, she was better able to put her thoughts into words. "Thank you for monitoring my ex. I can't do it. I get too obsessed, and it triggers my memories and makes him bigger in my life than I want him to be. But I did put an alert on DAVID, should anything hit the news regarding him."

"His escape has been hushed up. There's nothing in the news. It's embarrassing for the FBI and the United States to have lost him."

Ang had been busted for importing drugs into Honolulu and his U.S. holdings confiscated. His obsession with hunting Sophie down had ultimately led to his capture; but, as she'd feared, he'd been extradited to Hong Kong to stand trial—and hadn't even made it there.

"I would appreciate your help in finding him. But for any further action..."

"Fine. I hear you. But I won't promise to stay out of it entirely. Your safety matters to me."

"Fair enough," Sophie said.

Connor raised his hand and stroked the discolored, overly

tight skin graft on the side of her face—and she let him touch her there, the callouses on his fingertips slightly rough and his fingers warm.

His hand fell to his side.

She didn't know how to end things with him in this moment so they stood awkwardly, looking at each other, until Connor gave a small chuckle. "I like that about you, Sophie. You never try to fill the silence with unnecessary chatter."

"I wouldn't know how."

They walked to the door. He leaned toward her as if to kiss her again, but she turned her face so that his lips landed on her cheek.

She didn't know if she would be able to resist him if they kissed again, and she still didn't know what to do about his Ghost activities. "I'll see you when I go to Oahu next week, after the Hui contract is up. I have another laser graft surgery coming up."

"Pretty soon you won't even be able to tell…"

"That I was shot in the face?" Sophie smiled, but it felt like a tic. "You'll always be able to tell."

"Yes. And it doesn't matter." Before she could stop him, Connor kissed her—a quick stamp on her mouth that zinged right down to her toes. "I'll see you soon. And I'll let you know anything I find out about Ang."

"Thank you."

He lifted a hand and walked out. Sophie held the doorjamb, looking after him as he strode down the open walkway. She liked the set of his shoulders, the way he moved: elegant and disciplined. Connor was truly unique. "One in a million," Marcella would have said. *He was probably even more statistically unlikely than that.* She smiled, thinking of running a probability ratio on him through DAVID.

Sophie closed the door and locked it. That she had even

considered sleeping with a stranger who drank appletinis…thank God nothing had happened with that man.

Or Taggart.

Or, especially, Jake.

She went back to her computer and set DAVID to searching for anything to do with her ex, and, when she had done all that she could, she got into bed and called Marcella.

Bringing her FBI agent friend up-to-date on recent developments, including the fact that she was now included in the murder case, discharged some of the angst.

But she couldn't tell Marcella about Connor's role as the Ghost. Without that piece of information, explaining her ambivalence didn't make any more sense to Marcella than it had to Lei.

"You just need to sleep with him and get it over with. You'll know if he's the man for you after that," Marcella said. "It's that number Ang did on you when you were married. It's making you paranoid."

"And rightfully so. Assan tried to kill me. And he'll try again, if he can. Knowing he's free and could be anywhere in the world right now is not helping me relax." Sophie shivered in the warm wind that came through the window, then she got up to close and lock it. She took out her Glock and slid it under her pillow. "Time to go back to being Mary Watson. I'm moving out of here to a cash-only place tomorrow. This makes me realize that hiding from Assan was the real reason I came up with the Watson identity—even when he was in custody, I was afraid he'd find me again at my father's apartment."

"Ang will be more concerned about evading capture than finding you."

"I thought that about the last perp."

Marcella was silent at the reminder of the man who'd recently shot Sophie.

Often logic had nothing to with the urge to kill. Assan had already demonstrated his possessive need to own and control Sophie—and if he couldn't do that, to murder her.

"Keep your phone on. And don't worry. Between you and Todd, I have confidence that the two of you will find him online."

"Assan knows how to go off the grid and avoid cyber detection." Sophie didn't want to alarm her friend any further, so she downplayed the threat. "But he isn't as smart as we are. I'm sure we'll catch him soon."

"Well, I'm letting Marcus and Waxman know. I'll see what the FBI can do to help track him."

"Thanks. It can't hurt." Sophie ended the call. Knowing that her former Special Agent in Charge, Ben Waxman, and Marcella's dogged and powerful detective fiancé Marcus Kamuela would also be looking for her ex, gave her a measure of peace.

As she hung the blackout blankets over the windows and wrapped herself in the plumeria-print comforter, Sophie wished she had asked Connor to stay with her instead of showing him the door. She also missed her warm, faithful Labrador, Ginger. The dog was company—and an alarm system.

Instead, she was alone—and vulnerable.

Sleep took a long time to come.

Chapter 11

Sophie's phone, plugged in on the nightstand beside her bed, buzzed in an angry circle and woke her. She picked up immediately when she saw it was Lei.

"Someone burgled the crime scene," her friend said tersely. "Come down ASAP."

"Absolutely."

Tearing the blackout blankets off the windows, Sophie narrowed her eyes against the brilliant light reflecting off the water—it was already nine a.m., much later than she usually slept in. Fortunately, she had made headway on her probes into Magnuson and Mano's known associates, so she would have something to bring Lei in any case.

On the way to the Hui site she phoned Jake. It was past time to get her apology out of the way.

"Hey, girl." She'd know his playful baritone anywhere. "Hangover done yet?"

She groaned. "You know about that."

"I knew you were going to have a humdinger of one."

"Yes, it was terrible. I am shocked by how ill I was." Sophie paused to take a breath, blow it out. "I've never been really drunk before. My behavior was…"

"Don't mention it." Jake cut her off brusquely. "I know you're a lightweight. I could tell you stories, but you'd be embarrassed by them."

"I'm embarrassed already. I'm sorry for...the things I said." Sophie bit her lip, changing lanes on the Pi`ilani Highway to get past a slow-moving car before the road narrowed to two lanes around the cliffs to Lahaina, and she was stuck behind it. "It won't happen again."

"I told you, forget it." Jake's voice was rough, abrupt. He really didn't want to talk about it, and she didn't either. Once again, she envied the ease Lei had with Pono, but that didn't seem to be the dynamic she had with Jake.

"Okay, I won't mention it again. Some things have developed with the case. I'm going to be staying on Maui for the length of the Hui contract." Sophie told Jake about her new role supporting the murder investigation. "And now, Lei called me saying that the site has been burgled."

"What does that mean? A break-in at the trailer?"

"I don't know. I didn't take the time to ask." Sophie navigated around a truck and got behind another rental, settling into the traffic pattern that would take her into Lahaina. The stunning view of ocean trimmed in a lace of black rocks at the edge of the cliffs distracted her. "I'm on my way to the site now. I'll phone when I know more. Anything new on your job?"

"Our famous musician accepted Security Solutions' bid, so that's good news. And after your time with the Hui runs out, I'm hoping you'll be my partner on this job, too."

"Hmmm." Sophie frowned as she entered the short tunnel pierced through a particularly jagged crest of cliff. Per usual, cars honked and kids yelled out the windows. On this stretch of road on Maui, at least every other vehicle was occupied by a person on vacation and blowing off steam. "Setting up security for a celebrity isn't anything I know anything about, and this job has shown me I need more training."

Jake snorted. "Consider it on-the-job training. And yeah, we'll be screening, interviewing, and setting up bodyguards. Installing house and grounds alarms, even helping consult about some remodeling projects that will increase our guy's privacy. He even wants a trial with the A.I. nanny cam software that is Security Solutions' claim to fame...says he thinks someone on his current staff is selling him out."

"So when does the job begin?"

"I have to go back to Oahu, assemble the software and hardware, comb through our security personnel, and pick the best team for him and run ads if we don't have enough to cover the staffing. So, I'll be leaving soon. It's gonna take me a awhile to get it all together and come back to Maui, so the timing should work for you."

"Okay. Let me see this case through and then we'll discuss the situation with Bix." Sophie didn't want to commit yet. Living with Jake in a little guesthouse was a lot of being together in close proximity. "I have something else to tell you." She filled him in on what Connor had told her about Assan Ang's escape.

Jake exploded. "I can't believe the feds lost him! Damn incompetence!" He swore ripely.

"We don't know how he escaped," Sophie temporized. "We only know that he had help and that his escape was en route to Hong Kong.

"Todd has some Security Solutions' resources looking for him too. The more we know, the better we can be prepared." Her voice sounded brittle.

"Don't worry. We'll get this guy." Jake spoke forcefully.

"I hope so. Talk soon." She ended the call.

A few minutes later Sophie pulled up at the Kakela site,

parking the electric-blue Ford Fiesta rental under a spreading shade tree and locking it as she strode across the lot, frowning at the sight of the gate, its chain lock dangling and cut, leaving the entrance ajar.

Pomai Magnuson, wearing a fitted sheath dress in a hibiscus print, hair wound into a thick black bun pierced by a chopstick, was talking animatedly with Lei and Pono—and she stood beside two several deep, carelessly dug holes in the area that the GPR report had identified as possible burial sites.

Sophie's stomach tightened. Without her keeping an eye on the site, the burglar had been able to return, and deep, corrugated tracks digging into the soil from the gate showed that they'd driven a small backhoe in, dug the holes rapidly, and exited the same way. They'd probably loaded and unloaded the backhoe off a trailer. The yellow crime scene tape surrounding the body dump area lay shredded and strewn everywhere.

Pono had a black Canon camera out, photographing the scene.

This was no stealth operation—it was a blitz attack, as her former coach Alika would have called such a move in the MMA ring.

"Ms. Magnuson. I'm so sorry this happened!" Sophie exclaimed.

Pomai Magnuson turned. Her richly toned complexion was sallow, and the red lipstick on her full, pinched mouth had wandered on one side. "Ms. Ang. I'm sorry you weren't here monitoring the site, as your contract calls for."

"It was a crime scene now, and thus under MPD control," Lei intervened. "We met with Ms. Ang yesterday afternoon about the case. None of us thought the thieves would be back so soon after this place was filled with law enforcement personnel, or of course we would have had someone monitoring it!"

"Well, as I was telling you, these dig locations are almost surgically precise. The thieves knew where to dig and what they were looking for—and there's only one way that could happen. Someone got a copy of the ground penetrating radar report!"

Chapter 12

Brett Taggart's voice was harsh. "I have no idea how the thieves got the GPR report." He folded his arms across his chest and divided a glare between Lei and Pono, seated across from him at a steel table in one of the interview rooms at the Kahului Police Station.

"How many people have access to the GPR report?" Pono asked. Their voices came tinnily through the feed into the tiny observation room where Sophie sat. Pono was playing good cop, his usual role, Lei had told Sophie—but this was the first time she had actually seen their team in action. The big Hawaiian leaned forward, resting his thick forearms on the table as he addressed Taggart man-to-man. "We thought we'd talk with you first, because you're in charge of archaeology at the site."

Taggart imitated Pono's gesture by leaning forward onto his elbows on the table, but now the men were too close, and appeared to be locked into a confrontational stare. "You should be asking Pomai these questions. She's been plenty free with copies of the report and who she has given them to."

"Oh, we will. But first, we're interested in your copy of the report, and who has access to it," Lei said.

Sophie, watching this unfold, rubbed sweaty hands on her slacks. She could not be more grateful that her ill-advised flirtation with Taggart had only ended with a kiss. Lei and Pono had invited her to sit in on the interviews and come in and question the witnesses regarding security matters and the burglaries. Pomai Magnuson had identified that the thieves had been able to target identified densities of possible artifacts, thus pointing to the GPR report. The field of people who had access to that report was narrow, and began with Taggart.

* * *

Taggart had arrived at the site shortly after Sophie had, and had been as upset as she had ever seen him—his sharp-featured face had appeared drawn, his eyes hollow as he looked at the desecrated area. Careless piles of dirt surrounded the two large, jagged, slashed holes ripped deep into the ground. Splintered, rotten wood remained at the bottom of the hole.

The lights around the site had been shot out with something silent and accurate—broken bulbs dangled from the poles. The door of the trailer had been pried open and the monitoring equipment smashed. Sophie had left the cameras on after she left, and the thieves had taken care of the surveillance equipment in a way that was crude, but efficient. She had not been able to recover any usable images from the crushed recording devices.

Sophie traced the conical, cigar shape of a buried canoe on an interior page of her own copy of the GPR report, which she'd taken back to her condo after the body discovery.

Magnuson had been distraught about the destruction of the buried canoe. "This is where we think the queen might have been laid to rest," she had said at the site, dark eyes wide with anger.

"Because she drowned in the lagoon, we think that they may have put her body inside this canoe and buried it along with items special to her and the family. That the thieves got to it..." She had not even been able to finish her sentence, as tears welled in her eyes.

Now, his hands resting on the steel table, dirt still under his fingernails from climbing into the holes and trying to discern what might have been taken, that same outrage and grief was stamped on Taggart's face.

He was a very good actor if he was the one to sell out the location of the artifacts.

"I have my personal copy, which has not left my custody. My archaeological firm has theirs. I gave another copy to Sophie Ang with Security Solutions, and of course, the Hui has its own copy. Mine is kept under lock and key. But perhaps, someone broke into the trailer and stole the copy Sophie was given," Taggart said.

"Sophie says no. She took her copy with her when she left the site after the body was found. All right. Where were you between the hours of nine p.m. and six a.m.?" Lei asked.

"Sadly, in bed. Alone. Like I usually am." His voice was rueful.

"When was the last time you visited the site?"

"When the body was discovered. You can find my signature on the scene log. And also, when we found out about the desecration. I came to see how much of the excavation site had been disturbed by the crime scene team and the body dump. You know this perfectly well, because you met me there and already interviewed me."

"Can anyone verify your whereabouts last night?" Pono asked.

"I saw the landlady on my way to do laundry in the basement, but I'm afraid I don't have any other alibi. If you had asked me about the night before last, I would have had a much more interesting tale to tell."

Sophie felt her pulse lurch. *Was he going to disclose their meeting in the bar?*

But who cares if he did? Nothing had happened. So what if two lonely single people ran into each other at a bar and had a drink—and a kiss. She would tell Lei about it herself.

Pono raised his brows. "I'm listening."

"I went to a bar and found some female company that I took home. Just so you don't think I always do laundry at night for entertainment." His ironic tone made Pono chuckle.

So he hadn't left the bar alone as he'd told her he was going to...either that, or he was lying. Either way, Taggart didn't want to seem like he couldn't 'get laid' in front of the detectives.

The conclusion shrank Sophie's respect for the archaeologist. *What was wrong with doing laundry and going to bed at nine p.m.?* She did that kind of thing most nights, and it had never occurred to her that it wasn't perfectly normal.

Lei shifted in her chair. "All of this is beside the point. What matters is where you were last night. Did you do any archaeology work for the Hui yesterday? Have any idea who or what might be behind these burglaries?"

"Pomai and I met to discuss the offer from Blackthorne Industries to buy the Kakela site. We went over the offer—and it's quite a proposal. Includes a whole excavation and restoration plan, things that would take the Hui a decade to raise the funds for. Pomai had given me a copy of the proposal so I shared that with my boss and another supervisor, and we talked about what our recommendations were going to be to the Hui board regarding the offer. So yes, I was doing work for the Hui, but not on-site. It's a closed crime scene, remember?" Taggart's sharp brown eyes pinned Lei. "Not that that means anything to the people who broke in."

"We're very sorry for the desecration at the site," Lei said, lowering her voice and holding Taggart's gaze. "Personally, I'm just sick about it. I really wish we had kept Sophie in the trailer and even put a uniform on the place as well, to watch it. We simply didn't anticipate the..." She paused, appearing to search for the right word. "Persistence and boldness that this perp has demonstrated. And we're still not entirely sure the murder, and the site desecration, are linked."

"Oh, they're linked." Taggart leaned forward and spread his workman's hands on the table. "You just have to find out how."

"Do you have any idea how they're linked?"

"Aren't you the detectives? I'm just a glorified ditchdigger," Taggart barked.

"Have you ever heard of 'taking a bag'?" Lei's voice was conversational. "I only ask because I've heard it's a known shortcut between unscrupulous developers when they find a burial, and archaeologists willing to look the other way."

Taking a bag? Sophie had no idea what Lei was talking about, but the effect on Taggart was noticeable as the man's eyebrows shot up and he straightened in his chair. "Where did you hear that?"

Lei shrugged. "It's just a rumor I've heard. Sometimes, when a contractor is in a hurry and doesn't want to jump through all the hoops presented by finding an artifact or a burial on a property slated for development, they will offer a bag—meaning, a bag of cash—to the archaeologist doing the investigation. To look the other way, and speed up the process."

"I don't know where you've heard this, but it's bullshit."

Sophie worried at her lip, wishing she had her computer to

run a quick search on that phrase, see if she could unearth any documented cases of that kind of bribery.

Pono picked up the thread of the questioning next. "One of the things that we're hearing is that Mano had a lot of enemies. He was known to be a man with a little black book. Are we going to find your name on that list?"

Little black book? Sophie had only heard that phrase in connection with dating. Neither detective had said anything to Sophie about this discovery on Mano—it must've come out in their canvassing and other interviews. There was just no substitute for old-fashioned police work for uncovering some of the most important material on a case, and Sophie was forcefully reminded that she was not a part of that.

Taggart's face seemed to have frozen. His cynical dark eyes flicked between Lei and Pono. "Little black book? I don't know what you're talking about, but I don't like what you are implying."

Pono leaned forward, sympathetic. "It's understandable if you took a bag. Your company really doesn't pay you enough for the expertise that your job calls for, and there are all sorts of extra challenges that no one would think of here in Hawaii—the high cost of gas, the price of a rental, how much a drink costs at a bar to meet a woman."

Taggart folded his hands on the table. "I think this is the part where I ask for a lawyer."

"Before we get to that, I wonder if you could answer a few questions for our associate, Sophie Ang. She's helping us with the part of the investigation pertaining to the burglaries," Lei said.

Sophie blew out a breath. She had hoped, greatly, that she would not have to do this. She got up and walked around to the interview room door, opened it, and went inside. Taggart's eyes flashed with something dark—and regretful.

Sophie wished she knew exactly what it was, but she had never been that good at reading people. Maybe he was just embarrassed about those moments in the bar, and about how they were having this moment now.

"Hi, Dr. Taggart. I'm assisting MPD on this investigation as a private contractor. In the course of our background checks, we came across some information about your financials."

Taggart narrowed his eyes. "Don't you need a warrant for any of my private information?" The man knew his rights. She was going to have to tread carefully or DAVID's involvement would come under scrutiny.

"All of this is public record." Which was true. DAVID just accelerated its discovery. "I'd like to ask you about..." Sophie looked at the yellow-lined pad she had brought in. "A certain cash payment for a piece of property on the Big Island."

"Family inheritance. Not that it's any of your business." Taggart's gaze could not have been colder.

"I'm not sure about that," Pono said, shaking his head ruefully as he looked at a note inside the file in front of him. "We called your mother. We checked if there had been any large bequests in your family, because we thought perhaps that was a reason for the purchase."

"This was money from my dad's side. My parents are divorced. I didn't tell my mother because..." Taggart hunched his shoulders. "Because it would hurt her that she didn't have anything to leave me. If you call my father, he can verify that I inherited that money from an uncle."

Yes, if Brett Taggart was lying, he was a good actor.

"We'd like that number," Lei said. "Please."

"Sure." Taggart scrolled through his phone and rattled the number off.

"And we'd like your work and personal computer. To verify

you didn't have correspondence with Mano, or anything shady going on. We just want to rule you out," Pono said.

Taggart narrowed his eyes. "And you can have them when I get a warrant. I believe I asked for a lawyer."

Lei smiled, conciliatory. "No need to get so huffy. This is just a preliminary interview. You'll know when you need to get a lawyer." She stood, signaling the end of the interview, and extended her hand to Taggart. "Thanks so much for your cooperation."

Taggart shook Lei's hand perfunctorily, but his eyes were hard on Sophie as he did so. The two detectives preceded them to the door. Taggart came around the table and approached Sophie. "I'm quite interested in how you got hold of my financials," Taggart said, his hand clamping around her elbow. "Drinking buddy."

Sophie shook him off, refusing to meet his eyes. "I've signed confidentiality agreements. I cannot discuss the case with anyone but the immediate investigators."

"I think I have a right to know how you got that information. Given your computer skills, I suspect that it wasn't good old-fashioned police work that got the cops this far up my ass."

Sophie opened the door and speeded up once in the hallway, stretching long legs to catch up with Lei and Pono out in the hall.

"This makes me really glad we didn't sleep together," Taggart called loudly after her, and Sophie cringed as both Lei and Pono turned to look at her.

"Something you want to tell us?" Lei asked.

"I guess I have to," Sophie said. "Can we go somewhere private? It will only take a minute."

In the detectives' cubicle, she filled them in on her disastrous trip to the bar. Pono clapped her on the shoulder. "Well, you can be glad that at least Taggart didn't lie and say you slept together. He could have tried to smear you with that."

"Yes, I suppose so. But remember, he told me he was going home after I—said no. And then he told you he took someone else home from the bar. So he's a liar."

Pono smiled. "Most men are, when it comes to getting laid."

Lei snorted. "Stop it, Pono. You're going to put her off men, and she's already about as gun-shy as anyone can get."

"Sorry, Sophie. Men are dogs when it comes right down to it, and it's best you know that up front," Pono said. "But there are still some good ones out there. Loyal hound dogs that would follow you to the ends of the earth, and protect you with their life."

Lei socked Pono in the arm. "That's not sexy at all."

"It kind of is," Sophie said. "I wouldn't mind such a one." But could she navigate a relationship like that? Another question entirely.

* * *

Pomai Magnuson sipped from a sleek steel coffee carafe. Her polished nails flicked through a stack of papers inside a file she had carried in to the interview. Her demeanor was alert but relaxed. Clearly she felt she had nothing to fear from Lei and Pono, who sat on one side of the table as she and Sophie sat on the other.

"I brought along a copy of the offer and proposal from Blackthorne Industries," Magnuson said. "I thought...I don't know. Maybe some of the information in this report came from Mano. Maybe Mano was secretly brokering this deal with Blackthorne, and it has something to do with his death."

Sophie saw the electricity of interest move through both Lei and Pono, and she felt it herself: a tightening of the abs. A spike in her heart rate. There was a sense of being on point, catching a dangerous scent that brought a sharpening of all her senses. *Yes, tracking killers was addicting.*

"Who benefits from a deal with Blackthorne?" Lei asked, taking the report that Magnuson handed her.

"Well, the realtor handling the sale," Magnuson said. "And, as you may be aware, Mano owns his own real estate and development brokerage. Another person benefiting would be the architectural firm who gets the contract to complete the excavation and direct the restoration of the site." She leaned over with a pen and tapped several highlighted passages. "As you can see, a whole reconstruction of the original island's buildings and points of interest is planned. An architectural firm would be directing all of that recreation for historical accuracy. And of course, the Hui would benefit, with a tremendous influx of cash. We could go on to excavate and restore another worthy site, and we have one in mind."

Lei tilted her head and smiled. There was a hunter's gleam in her wide, clear brown eyes. "You realize you have just provided yourself with motive."

"Oh, I realize that." Magnuson flapped her hand. "But I do not directly benefit from any of this. My salary from the Hui is fair, but small potatoes for the director of a historical nonprofit. And my job is secure, no matter what happens with this site...I benefit from none of this in any financial way."

"But perhaps there is something other than financial," Pono said.

Magnuson speared him with a contemptuous glance. "I dare you to find a reason for me to sabotage my job." She seemed personally offended, and Sophie remembered that Pono had mentioned that she and his wife were friends.

"Then perhaps you wouldn't mind submitting your work and home computer to us for a quick search. Just to rule you out as a suspect," Lei said.

Magnuson's large dark eyes flared wide. "That's…awfully invasive. But I have nothing to hide. Sure, take them."

"Good. Sophie will accompany you back to the Hui's office and collect it, and your home computer, too," Lei said.

"Fine." Magnuson bit off the word. "Do you have any more questions for me?"

"Yes. We have already searched Mano's home and collected his computer. Did he have a workstation or computer he used at the Hui's offices? Because we will want to go through those, too."

"He did. There is a neutral workstation set up in the Hui's library area that all the board members can use."

"All right, we'll come with you and search that area, and Sophie will take that computer in for analysis as well."

Following Magnuson's stiff back down the hall of MPD, Sophie wished that she'd met this woman some other time—they might have become friends. It seemed impossible they ever could be now.

* * *

A wide, shallow box held a large bag of soil in the king's hidden room. He turned on one of the spotlights trained upon it and approached. Wearing latex gloves, the king reached his hands into the earth inside the bag. Even through the gloves, he could feel mana infusing the very earth of his ancestors' burial place. He wished, in this moment, that he could touch the soil uncovered, sift through it and find her bones with his bare hands—but the oils from his skin could corrupt the bone, and that wasn't something he wanted to risk.

The king gently sifted the soil from one bag to another, handful by handful. Shreds of wood from the disintegrating hull of the canoe that had held her, fragmented in his hands.

The first bone he found was a slender, straight humerus, its color stained by the earth to a deep, rich red-brown. One by one, he removed her bones from the dirt as he found them, setting them in a pile on one side of the table and clearing the soil from one bag into another.

The king regretted the crudeness of her removal from her grave. He would make up for it in the future.

A bone hook that must have been a pendant around her neck was caught on the fragile arc of her clavicle. The king used a soft brush to remove the soil, keeping the two objects connected as he lifted the clavicle out of the soil and gently laid it on the pile.

He removed the bone hook.

The hook was a decorative style, not the simple arc with detachable barbs used for serious fishing. This one was a graceful crescent, the point curled inward, sharp and yet appealingly smooth. Mana seemed to emanate from it, calling to him, and the king could not resist.

He stripped off his latex gloves and cradled the hook in his hands, leaning down to breathe on it. He wondered why the impulse to do that was so strong, but did not question the need to do it again, breathing over it three times.

Making sure the hook was clear of dirt, he walked over to the drawer where its place awaited, a nest of black velvet. Setting the hook in the drawer, gazing at it, then closing it away with his other treasures gave him a deep sense of satisfaction.

Returning to the bag of soil, he removed the rest of the skeleton. His amateur study of archaeology and genealogy made the moment particularly poignant and personal.

The king was exhuming the skeleton of his great ancestress, the queen. This was the high point of his quest, and he paused to savor it as he reassembled her skeleton on the nearby table, covering her with an ornamental tapa cloth. Here she would wait, until the time was right to be returned to her resting place. And in the meantime, he would visit her every day.

Chapter 13

Sophie settled into a decent office chair in the MPD's computer lab. One other tech officer was working with her in the space, but per the norm, no conversation took place—both of them were already wired in. Sophie already had made a clone copy of the computer she wanted to begin searching with the MPD's write blocker. She began with the hard drive of Seth Mano's home computer—the one most likely to contain any secrets the man had.

The technology for cloning a computer took a while, so she settled in to work as the device worked on copying the hard drives of Pomai Magnuson's computers. Lei had also promised Sophie Brett Taggart's work and home computers to work on before the day was over.

Searching for any hidden files with a sifting program, Sophie soon located a suspicious QuickBooks file hidden under the title *Personal Accounts*. Scrolling through a list of payments, going back three years and only accompanied by initials, Sophie mused over the title of the file. When she looked at Mano's bank accounts, no corresponding record of the payments listed could be found. Sophie picked up the desktop phone and dialed Lei's extension.

"You better come down here."

Moments later, Lei leaned over Sophie's shoulder as Sophie showed her the list of payments. "Pono's out running down something for the case. What do you think these payments are?"

"Well, the initials are all different and the dates are all different, and the amounts are all different. But see?" Sophie pointed to the screen. "Many of these initials recur, either monthly or just every so often. And look at the amounts. Anything from five hundred to two thousand dollars. Nothing too huge, but they're consistent." Sophie glanced up at Lei. "I think we're looking at Mano's side job. He was a blackmailer." Sophie pushed her chair back so she could gaze at her friend. "Was this what you were referring to when you mentioned a 'black book' to Taggart?"

"Exactly." Lei sat down in an office chair beside Sophie. "One of the witnesses we interviewed about Mano, an associate at his firm, implied that Mano dealt in information—that he supplemented and strengthened his real estate development business through shady dealings. I wasn't sure what that meant until now."

"Well, do you think any of these initials match possible blackmail victims? Victims who might have turned against Mano? Unfortunately, there are a lot of initials here."

Lei shook her head. "I hope it will be easier than that. All we need to find is someone involved with the Hui whose initials are also on this list. It's unlikely that a completely unrelated blackmail victim would have chosen to meet Mano at the Kakela site."

Sophie turned back to the computer and began to scroll. "Let's begin by looking for PM and BT." They scrolled through, but none of the known board members or staffers' initials were on the list. "Unfortunately, we have to consider the possibility that these initials are coded," Sophie said. "He could have an additional decoding key stored elsewhere. It would make sense with how relatively easy this file was to find. And another thing—have you considered that there must be a cache where he keeps the materials to back up his blackmail?"

"We've already searched his home, and we have a warrant to get into his safe deposit box. The tricky thing is that he didn't have a central place where all of his accounts and bank information were stored. I had to hunt for it with the help of his housekeeper."

"So Mano was single?"

"A widower. Wife died two years ago. Cancer."

"By the timing, the blackmail began a year before her death. I wonder if this blackmail business is related somehow," Sophie said.

Lei was working her phone with her thumbs. "I'm updating Pono on all this."

"I have always thought that knowing motive can help give us a clear idea of who benefits from the crime. In a situation like this, knowing why Mano was blackmailing could help point to his killer."

Lei glanced at Sophie. "In this case, I think we should stay focused on concrete police work, like finding the decryption key and tracking down these initials. I would like that file emailed to me so Pono and I can include it in Mano's case jacket, and discuss it with Captain Omura."

Sophie nodded, accepting her friend's leadership on the case.

"And I have some other news." Lei spun back and forth in her chair to discharge the same sort of restless energy that Sophie felt on occasion. "Pono and I met with Dr. Gregory over at the medical examiner's office. Mano was killed with the rock we identified. Cause of death was blunt force trauma."

"No surprise there." Sophie raised her brows.

"No, but he found an unidentified hair stuck in Mano's blood on the body. We ran it already—not in the system. But if we can locate that person, we have some good forensic evidence to close the case."

* * *

Sophie was still sifting through the next computer when Pono carried in a box containing two more. "The warrant came through for Taggart's computer," he said, setting the heavy box down on the table next to her work area. Sophie blinked up at him. Her eyes felt gritty from staring at the screen for hours. The external sound-sensing feature on her headphones had muted the concerto she was listening to when Pono spoke to her.

"Hey, how long have you been down here?" Pono said, surveying the dimly lit room. The other officers had left long ago.

Sophie pushed back her chair and leaned back to stretch. "Not sure."

"Well, it's quitting time." He pointed at the small, square write blocker device. "Why don't you get that thing going, and come home with me for a home-cooked meal while it clones Taggart's hard drive? You can always come back here after, if you're feeling the urge to be a workaholic."

Sophie's stomach rumbled in agreement with that plan. "That sounds perfect," she said gratefully. "I'd be happy to accept."

Pono rattled off his address and she captured it with the notes feature on her phone.

It wasn't long before she was sitting down to a meal that the frighteningly capable Tiare Kaihale had "just thrown together."

Sophie picked up her spoon and dug into a savory beef stew

laden with chunks of pineapple and Molokai sweet potato ladled over a mountain of dense, sticky white rice. Around the table, Ikaika and Maile, Pono and Tiare's children, partook with equal gusto.

"So...how are you kids doing?" Sophie asked. She hadn't spent much time aroundschool-age children, and wasn't sure how to engage with them. "What are your interests?"

Young Ikaika, Pono's boy child, piped up. "I got moved to forward position on my soccer team," he said proudly, cheeks bulging with a bite of stew. Maile, not to be outdone, added that her hula halau was competing in the children's division finals at the Merrie Monarch hula festival on the Big Island next year.

Sophie smiled, listening to and watching the lively by-play of the family around the table. Tiare's work as a nurse at the hospital kept her busy, but not so busy that she hadn't started another business as a wedding planner, in addition to helping teach hula and being active in the couple's church. As the meal concluded, Sophie touched Pono on the arm. "You are a lucky man," she said. "Never forget it."

Pono smiled, that big white grin she was becoming fond of. "Not just lucky. Blessed. And grateful, every day."

* * *

Sophie unbuckled her seatbelt as the short Hawaiian Airlines flight from Maui parked at the gate in Honolulu Airport.

She had barely had time to boot up her laptop and begin to take a look at the cloned hard drive of Brett Taggart's computer. It had not been worth the effort to boot the thing up when the flight was a mere thirty minutes, but she had not been able to resist the lure of at least having a quick look at his hard drive, searching for anything to do with the Kakela site.

And of course, it was not enough time to do anything but determine that Taggart was not a very organized record-keeper on his PC.

A twinge of apprehension tightened her abs as Sophie made her way down the jetway to the exit. She did not have a checked bag, only the backpack she carried for the quick overnight trip back to Oahu to fulfill her laser scar removal treatment. Security Solutions' VP Bix was picking her up, and she wasn't particularly looking forward to it.

Bix was driving one of the white Honda SUVs that were part of Security Solutions' fleet of vehicles, each equipped with a removable magnetic logo on the doors. Jake had told her that the company had used market research to decide what kind of vehicle to buy in bulk in Hawaii, and white Honda CRVs were the answer. They looked like they were owned by people who resided on the island, but were anonymous enough not to attract attention.

"Welcome home," Bix said, as she slid into the passenger seat and pushed her backpack into the rear.

"Thank you for picking me up."

"An in-person situation report was overdue." Bix was all business, as usual. Her supervisor was dressed down in chinos and a polo shirt, but he would have fit in easily at the FBI with his clean-cut style and no nonsense, protocol-driven mindset.

"I agree. I want to sort through some of the things that have been happening, and get your advice as far as my evolving role in the murder investigation," Sophie said.

"Good. Let me take you to lunch."

Sophie hadn't eaten that morning, still full fromTiare's delicious stew, but her early morning run, along beautiful Sugar Beach outside of the cash-only condo she had taken under the Mary Watson identity, had helped burn calories, and now she was hungry again.

It was remarkable and annoying to her how the body kept requiring fuel, no matter how much turmoil the emotions were in.

They went to Zippy's, a local chain restaurant, and Sophie unburdened herself about the case, telling Bix from start to current situation how things were going.

"I worry that you are becoming indispensable to this investigation, and your priorities as a hired security agent, are becoming blurred. It is MPD's investigation now. The Hui's contract with us ends in a few days. They have no purpose in continuing the contract, since, as you pointed out, the site has already been looted."

"Literally, on my watch," Sophie said ruefully as she poked at the Caesar salad with ahi strips she had ordered. "I was shocked that Magnuson didn't fire me after that happened. I think Lei talked them into keeping me on."

"Well, you always have to keep in mind now that you are a private contractor, and your priority is what the client pays you for," Bix said. His jaw was a tight line. "You're done with that case the minute your contract expires."

"Absolutely." The word tasted like sawdust in Sophie's mouth.

* * *

Sophie swished down another pain pill outside of Connor Remarkian's swanky Pendragon Arches apartment—the laser treatment to minimize the edges of her skin graft had left her face swollen and achy. Not the best time to see him, but one or the other of them had been recovering from wounds for the duration of their relationship.

She rang the bell, glancing at the overhead surveillance cam in the hall, remembering the first time she'd stood outside this door. She was never sure if he would answer the door, or his assistant, or even if it would be a maid—but today it was Connor himself, and his face lit up at the sight of her. She had always wondered about that American phrase, wondered what it meant, what it would look like to see. The widening of his eyes and the broad smile that transformed Connor's face was a clear answer.

"I wondered if I would see you again, after our talk on Maui," Connor said. "Come in."

Sophie stepped across the threshold, and he hugged her. She sighed as she relaxed into him, the physical touch a balm to her jangled nerves and the pain that haunted her from unhealed wounds.

Finally, she stepped back. "I hunted you for too long for you to get rid of me that easily," she said. "I need your help. I'm here on island for a personal medical reason, but I need a secure place to use DAVID for the investigation."

If Connor was disappointed, he hid it well. He closed the door behind her and locked it as Anubis, his dignified Doberman, sniffed at Sophie and thrust his head under her hand for a pet. She stroked Anubis's silky head, touching the tips of his cropped, pointed ears with a delicate hand. She missed Ginger. She was definitely going to spend the night at her place, and pick up her dog from the kennel where she'd been boarding the Lab.

"We will need to use my secure work room, in that case."

"How often do you check for listening devices in here?" Sophie said.

"Daily. And the other side, twice a day." Connor smiled, and she wanted to kiss him. She wanted to *more* than kiss him. *But nothing had changed.* He was still the Ghost, she was still conflicted about that, and the closer they got, the more difficult it all became.

He led her through the immaculately appointed apartment into his bedroom—which might have been suggestive if she hadn't known that it was an entrance to his other world.

Soon they were sitting down in Connor's secret computer lab. Sophie opened her laptop and plugged it into his cable network. "I have never asked you what software you use for…those activities."

Connor was sitting next to her in a second ergonomic office chair. "I have a software program that has unique hacking abilities. And that's all I'm going to say on that subject."

"Does it have a name?"

Connor smiled. "Where do you think the name Ghost comes from?"

Sophie shook her head, smiling too. "I guess it's better not to know."

"Well, if something ever happens to me, I have the program stored in a safe deposit box. I will put you on as a cosigner."

Sophie turned to face him fully, seriousness pulling down her mouth. "Don't say that. I can't bear to hear you say that."

"It almost seems like you care." Connor's blue-green eyes were bleak.

"You know I care. That's why this hurts."

He swiveled his chair abruptly away, facing the bank of computers. "What I do with what's mine is my choice. You're the only one who knows about the Ghost, and I have to tell someone. I have to let someone in on all of this in case it all goes to shit…in case I'm caught."

"Stop it." Tears filled Sophie's eyes. "Please don't say that. Don't tell me this."

He shrugged, not looking at her. "It is what it is. Now, tell me what you've got here to work on."

Clearly he didn't want to talk about this minefield of a topic any longer. Sophie blew out a breath and refocused on the cloned hard drive she'd imported onto her laptop. She filled him in on getting it from Taggart. "I want to run a deep background on Taggart with DAVID while I'm searching this clone of his computer."

"Well, this is the most secure Internet location you could find, short of the Pentagon, and maybe more secure than that," Connor said. "I have some things to do, myself. Let's get to work."

Sophie nodded. She removed her Bose headphones from her bag and plugged them in, booting up the laptop, and set two powerful programs to work as her fingers flew over the keyboard.

It was remarkably companionable to sit beside Connor and work, both lost in their own digital worlds—together. *Equal.*

The hours rolled by quietly, and the longer Sophie spent in Connor's inner sanctum, the more it felt like home.

Sophie left the computer mining for information on Taggart's cloned hard drive while she and Connor went to dinner. Over a steak and a glass of a good Merlot at a restaurant within walking distance of the apartment building, Connor lifted his glass.

"To great partnerships."

Sophie touched her glass to his, and enjoyed the chime of the crystal. "I like your office," she said. "I like working with you. And I don't say that to too many people. You know when to keep quiet."

Connor smiled. "I was going to say the same of you. A year ago, I would not have imagined letting anyone into my office, and now, I just know how much I'm going to miss you when you aren't there."

"I hate it when you say things like that. I feel like I don't know what to say back to you, like no matter what I say, it's the wrong thing. A disappointment." Sophie sipped her wine to hide the tremble of her lips.

"You're overthinking it. You can always just tell me what your first thoughts are, and I am always glad to know what they are."

Sophie ducked her head and tugged at the curls that were still too short to cover the angry-looking skin graft that marred her temple.

Connor switched to lighter topics, and they discussed the politics of the Internet and ended up on the case that Sophie was investigating. "It was a breakthrough to get Mano's record of blackmail payments," Sophie said. "But I think it is a coded file. The initials don't match anyone we know that had contact with Mano."

Connor's smile was deadly. "Ghost can crack that code. Give me the file when we get back to the apartment."

Back at the apartment, Sophie transferred the file to a stick drive and gave it to Connor. "I'm sure I'm not supposed to be doing this, even though you are my boss. I signed confidentiality agreements with the MPD. But I think this is the fastest way for us to get answers that will break this thing open."

Connor nodded. "Agreed."

While Connor got his software working on the blackmail file, Sophie reviewed Taggart's hard drive. An hour or so later, she had identified the ground penetrating radar report. A residual signature showed the file had been copied. She surfed through Taggart's email and found the file sent to an anonymous numbered account. She set DAVID to apply a tracker program to uncover that destination, and it pinged back within minutes.

"I have a location for the computer that received a copy of the GPR report from Taggart's computer," Sophie said, breaking the deep and comfortable silence between them. "And it's here on Oahu."

Chapter 14

Sophie woke and rose from the pretty little rattan bed in her apartment, greeted rapturously by Ginger. The big yellow Lab could wag her tail with her whole body, and that was exactly what the big dog did, hopping and slobbering all over Sophie.

Sophie petted the Lab and padded into her little kitchen, plugging in the electric kettle for tea. In spite of the breakthrough last night, Sophie was dogged with a feeling of frustrated futility. Connor was still working on breaking the code of the blackmail file, and she'd kissed him good night and left, contacting Lei on Maui and sending her the IP location of the computer that had received Taggart's email of the GPR report.

Giving over that information but not being able to go on the raid to see what they unearthed reminded Sophie again of the limitations of being a private contractor.

She drank her tea and took Ginger out for a run. Soon she was jogging on the beach at Ala Moana Park with the dog. The chattering of mynah birds and doves waking up in the park, the morning sun glittering off of the tall, mirrored high-rises of Waikiki, and a little wind picking up across the turquoise water all soothed her spirits.

At least she and Connor were getting along, and he was confident he'd have the blackmail list code broken soon. Working together, the lovely dinner, and Connor's goodnight kiss—tempting enough to want to make her stay the night—all warmed her, but second thoughts about leaving the FBI still nagged at her.

Her phone rang in her pocket, and Sophie trotted over to stand under a palm tree and pick up for Lei. "Sophie, I'm on my way to Honolulu, but I've been hung up by some personal business. I need you to go on the raid of that address you found with the Honolulu Police Department staff—a Sergeant Chimes will be in charge. Confiscate any computer equipment you find and get started searching it. And I'll be there by noon."

"Thanks," Sophie said. "I really needed this." Her heart rate was already up, the cobwebs of incipient depression dismissed by the excitement of the hunt.

"I'm not doing it for you," Lei said with a dry chuckle. "I'm doing what's best for the case. Even if that means I don't get to be there for the takedown."

* * *

Sophie picked up another call without checking the caller ID as she ran hard for her apartment.

"Sophie, where are you?" Jake's voice was short. "I went by your condo on my way to the airport. I'm on Oahu now."

"I'm on Oahu too, and I'm in a hurry, Jake. What do you want?" Sophie panted, clattering up the exterior stairs of her apartment. "I'm getting ready for a raid."

"You could have told me you were leaving the island." Jake sounded irritated.

"We aren't even on the same job. I don't owe you an

explanation for anything," Sophie said, her temper flaring to match his. "I had personal medical business on Oahu, and some things are breaking on the case."

"Partners keep each other informed," Jake said, each word measured and controlled. "And I'm calling with some news from your case as well."

Sophie unlocked her apartment hastily and pushed in, hauling Ginger behind her. "Go ahead."

"I went by the Kakela site to check in with you, and met Magnuson. She informed me that the board has rejected the offer from Blackthorne Industries."

"That's interesting, but likely irrelevant," Sophie said, stripping off her clothes and heading for the shower as Ginger lapped thirstily from her water bowl.

"Well, I thought I would pass it on, in case it was of value or interest." Jake's tone was frosty. "What's breaking on your end?"

"Sorry, Jake, I have to shower and get down to HPD for a raid. I'll update you later." Sophie ended the call and set the phone on the edge of the sink, jumping into the shower.

Under the flow of water, soaping briskly, she thought about the Blackthorne offer. It seemed unrelated to the case, but there was no way to tell with the current information they had.

It took her fifteen minutes to change and get to the HPD headquarters downtown and to connect with the sergeant in charge of the raid. Soon Sophie, wearing standard black Kevlar and a helmet, was careening through the streets of downtown Honolulu in the SWAT SUV, headed for the building whose address contained the computer she had found.

Breath constricted by the vest, vision narrowed by the dark helmet, ears filled with the buzzing static of the comm, Sophie jogged after the SWAT team up the interior stairs of the apartment building. The address had been identified as a corner unit on the fourth floor—but when the squad leader knocked on the door, there was no answer.

"Open up! Honolulu Police Department!"

No reply.

Two of the officers wielded the door cannon, and the apartment was breached with two blows. Sophie hung back, per protocol, her weapon drawn as she kept an eye on the hallway and the officers went into the unit.

"Clear!"

"Clear!"

Sophie listened to them checking in as they scanned the interior rooms, and she entered at their signal.

The apartment was a bland and uninteresting interior office space, done in shades of industrial beige and gray. A series of modular metal office furnishings, their drawers hanging open and file cabinets empty, testified to having been hastily vacated—but several older computers still dotted the room, and Sophie pointed to them. "I need all of those."

* * *

Sophie sat at the long rectangular conference table in one of the conference rooms at Honolulu Police Department. Ranged around the table were Marcella's fiancé, Marcus Kamuela, Lei, and Chimes, the sergeant in charge of the SWAT unit. Sophie had set her write blockers to work copying the hard drives of the confiscated computers during the meeting.

"The fact that the office was empty and quickly abandoned points to someone monitoring the situation and being able to pull out before detection," Sergeant Chimes said. He was a husky mixed Hawaiian and looked ready for business, still dressed in SWAT black. "According to the building manager, the office was a month-to-month lease from a company that paid cash. The manager saw employees come and go, and a lot of activity this last Friday. But it never seemed like anything suspicious. According to him, Smith Enterprises did telemarketing."

"Telemarketing is the perfect cover for a money laundering or gambling front," Kamuela said. "The lack of supplies going in or out is explained by the nature of the supposed business."

"So why would this shell company have wanted the GPR report from Taggart? And why would he have given it to them?" Lei asked.

"I think we will have to ask Taggart that," Sophie said, rubbing the scar on her cheek as it tingled uncomfortably, a side effect from the laser treatment. "And as to why, that is how that latest burglary attempt was able to pinpoint the location of artifacts and extract them. Once I get these computers pulled apart, I hope to be able to determine how they knew we were coming, and where the report went from here."

* * *

The afternoon passed relatively peacefully for Sophie as she searched through the office computers' hard drives. She finally called it a day at around seven p.m. and contacted Lei on her cell. "These computers were empty. That whole raid was a total waste of time and effort. Whoever cleared out the offices took the computer that received the GPR file with them."

"I'm not getting anywhere with my leads, either," Lei said. "Let's meet Marcella for a drink."

"Sounds perfect."

Duke's by the Beach was a classic surfer-themed restaurant bar. Over loaded potato skins and bottles of beer, the three women compared personal notes. Marcella flashed the sparkling diamond engagement ring her fiancé Marcus Kamuela had given her.

"I told Marcus not to get me some ridiculous rock, but the man never listens." Marcella said, fussing with the ring, but the pink in her cheeks told Sophie that she liked the ostentatious diamond in spite of her complaint. "My biggest worry is that it will catch on something during a case. I hardly ever wear it during the day."

Lei held out her hand, decorated with a practical band of small, channel-set diamonds. "I can wear this one pretty much anywhere. Stevens knew I wouldn't tolerate some big rock— sorry, Marcella."

Sophie waggled her bare hand. "Meanwhile, your single friend is barely dating."

"I don't know. If I had to choose between Connor and Jake, with Alika on the side, I am not sure who I would pick." Marcella bounced her brows and grinned.

Sophie snorted. "Alika is out of the picture and Jake is my partner, and that's all. And Connor?" Sophie smiled. "Well, Connor is a very good kisser."

The other women toasted to Sophie's new relationship. "But I don't know how things can progress very well between his schedule and mine," Sophie said. "When this case is over, which it will be when my contract runs out at the end of the week, it looks like my next job is on Maui, too, and will likely be pretty immersive as we develop security for a rock star who is being stalked. I don't know how much time I'll even have to see Connor."

"But you'll have plenty of time with Jake," Marcella said, elbowing Sophie.

Sophie just shook her head, sipping her beer.

"Quit giving her a hard time, Marcella," Lei said. "I'm sure it's not easy having a hot, single partner who's attracted to you—let's not lie during girl-time. Jake's into you. An idiot could see that, and it makes me so glad Pono and I always had the brother and sister dynamic going on. He nags, fusses like a mother hen, and we end up finishing each other's sentences—but I've never had to deal with any weird feelings or mind games. That cannot be fun."

Sophie nodded. "Yes. Jake called me just this afternoon and was upset that I hadn't told him I was going to Oahu, when it was clearly none of his business." She stabbed her fork into a potato skin and cut it so vigorously that she jiggled the table. "That reminds me. I never got back to him about the raid. But frankly, his behavior is..." Sophie shrugged and focused on eating, eyes on her plate. It was hard to put into words the complicated feelings she had for Jake—sometimes like a brother, sometimes like a friend, and sometimes...*something else.*

Marcella shook her head. "Yeah, I guess you're right. My partner, Matt Rogers, couldn't be more married. When I was single, it was annoying that he always wanted to get off work on time and get home for a meal with his wife, put his daughters to bed—but now I realize that's a much more balanced way to live."

"Absolutely." Lei dabbed her mouth with a napkin. "Being home with Stevens and Kiet is the high point of my day. I don't know why I was so phobic about making a commitment for so long."

"You two are not helping. I'm not sure how much I want to get involved with Todd..." Sophie swallowed past the lump in her throat of all she couldn't tell her friends about Connor.

"He's perfect for you!" Lei said. "I can't imagine a better partner for a computer workaholic who loves fitness like you."

Frustration and sadness at the necessary omission of the reason for her ambivalence tightened Sophie's throat. She could see why they thought he was perfect for her—and he was, except for the one, giant, glaring problem—*the Ghost.* "We will just have to see how it goes."

Chapter 15

The next morning, Sophie woke to the second hangover of her life. "Not again. Never doing this again." She groaned, and rolled to the side of the bed, setting her feet carefully on the floor. Ginger reached up to lick her face with an eager tongue, and the sensation sent Sophie running to the bathroom. She managed not to vomit, but it took a few minutes of deep breathing for her stomach to settle. She rinsed her furry mouth and brushed her teeth, hoping to get her energy flowing again.

Several cups of tea later, Sophie picked up her phone and checked her messages. Connor had left a text: *cracked the code on the blackmail list. Come get it. Also, I missed you last night.*

Sophie texted back. *Absence makes the heart grow fonder, Americans say. Just putting that theory to the test. I will be by in an hour.*

An hour seemed ambitious to feel better, so she texted Marcella: *got any hangover cures?* Marcella had some ideas, and several aspirins and a bottle of orange juice later, Sophie showed up at Connor's apartment with Ginger in tow.

"Got any hair of the dog to put in here?" Sophie held up the jug of orange juice she was sipping on. "Marcella told me to ask you for some. Said you'd know what that meant, and that it wasn't hair from Ginger."

Connor broke into a grin. "You've come to the right place, my hungover friend." He led her to a wet bar concealed in one of the cabinets of the room's sleek, modern decor. "A dash of vodka in that OJ ought to fix you up."

"Yes. This is what Marcella recommended as the final part of my hangover cure." Sophie sipped at the concoction, and grimaced. "I went out with my friends last night, and I'm really not a drinker. I didn't even have any alcohol at my apartment to do the hair of the dog with."

"Well, you certainly brought a hairy enough animal," Connor said as Ginger rapturously fawned over Anubis. The two dogs wagged and sniffed, and even frolicked a little in the spacious living room. "I copied the blackmail list onto the stick drive. Do you want to go back to the Batcave and work on it?"

Sophie's first smile of the day felt good. "The Batcave is a good name for your office. I should probably just hand the list straight over to Lei, but I can't wait to dive into it and cross-check the initials you uncovered with the names of everyone we've associated with the case so far."

Connor's secret office was as cool and peaceful as she remembered it, and putting on her headphones and diving into the wired universe through the secure rig Connor had set up for her felt like finding an unexpected haven. She loaded the name file she had already created that included all of the employees of the Hui, everyone they had so far uncovered associated with Mano's murder case, and all of Mano's known business associates, though Sophie was prepared to find out that list did not reflect half of the scope of whatever his activities had been.

It didn't take long for the list to ping with several names—

and one of them raised Sophie's brows. "Got a name here that Lei is going to be very interested in."

"Going to share?" Connor slanted a blue-green glance at her.

"I can't. We have confidentiality agreements. But I'll tell you as soon as I can, and you are overdue for a thank-you." Sophie got up and rotated Connor's chair so he was facing her, and before she could second-guess herself, she climbed onto his lap and straddled him, ignoring his surprised intake of breath.

Taking Connor's face in her hands, Sophie kissed him.

Oh, so good.

She seemed to sink into him, and he into her. He tasted of coffee and passion, and sensation zipped up and down Sophie's spine, tingled over her skin, and softened her heart. Connor's arms around her gave her the same sense of a surprising haven that the computer work area he'd made for her had wrought.

She kissed him some more.

Connor finally broke their embrace, looking up at her. "That's some thank-you. Want to continue this…elsewhere?"

Sophie smiled. "I have to get this information to Lei. And I don't want to rush whatever comes next. This will just have to be a preview."

Connor squeezed her and stroked her. "Consider me hooked by this trailer, and eager for the opening night premiere."

Sophie touched his cheek and hopped up off of his lap. "I have to run. But keep my chair warm."

Connor's smile made her think of dawn breaking over Haleakala. "I'm going to hold you to that."

* * *

Lei danced a little jig in her borrowed cubicle at the HPD, holding the stick drive aloft. "You're amazing, Sophie, and whatever Security Solutions is paying you, it's not enough."

Sophie grinned. She hated taking credit for Connor's work, but it couldn't be helped. "I have often thought the same of you, Lei. But this has never been about the money, has it?"

Lei smiled back. "No. It hasn't, it's about the satisfaction of getting guys that need to get got."

Sophie couldn't help thinking of Connor's determined expression as he told her the why of the Ghost: *"because it needs to be done, and because I can."*

She and Lei did what they could, too.

Lei plugged the stick drive in to the departmental computer and booted up the list that Sophie had cross-checked. "Blackthorne? I thought Blackthorne Industries made an offer on the Kakela site."

"Yes, they did. After the site was burgled, that offer was rejected. My theory is that Mano sold out the GPR report to Blackthorne, and then tried to blackmail him. Blackthorne, or whoever was representing him, took matters into his or her own hands with the rock found on the premises—and I think it was a male perp because Mano's body would be hard for a woman to move from where he was killed in the parking lot, to the pit where the body was dumped."

Lei nodded. "That's a good working theory. If Blackthorne's behind the artifact looting, we should find some evidence of it at his home."

"He seems pretty well-connected. Will likely have legal representation," Sophie said.

"That's fine. With his name on this blackmail list, I'll have grounds to get the search warrant." Lei rubbed her hands together. "This won't take long. Go find the gear you used for the other raid. We're going on a field trip to search a mansion."

Chapter 16

Blackthorne's estate was a sprawling compound in the Kailua foothills. Lei, Sergeant Chimes, and Sophie barreled through winding roads over the mountain. As she always did, Sophie tried to steal glances at the sweeping views of the spectacular mountain range, corrugated and deeply green from the frequent rains. Huge albizia trees, draped in vines, provided shade and green cover over the spectacular highway, and wild ginger scented the air beneath.

But all too soon that drive was over, and they turned into an upscale neighborhood. Sophie was surprised when they ran out of development and continued on a small, winding, well-kept road flush with the mountains.

Sophie tightened down her Kevlar vest and pulled her hat low over short, thick curls. Her unmarked black SWAT gear seemed like something she should just keep in her car, as frequently as she was wearing it.

The sergeant drove confidently down the road. "The Blackthorne estate has been here close to a hundred years," he said. "They're one of our oldest missionary families. Got all this land back in the day before it was worth anything and have hung onto it ever since."

"Any local gossip you can tell us about Blackthorne?" Lei asked. Sophie liked how her friend was always alert for an investigative opening in conversation.

"He's a big philanthropist to Hawaiian causes. Supports Kamehameha schools and donates annually to the Bishop Museum. He's a good guy."

Sophie took a closer look at the man's pinched mouth as Lei narrowed her eyes. Clearly, the sergeant didn't like his current assignment.

"Does he have a family? Anyone we should be concerned about upsetting with this warrant?" Lei asked.

"He's divorced. No children."

"Do you know him socially?" Sophie asked on impulse.

Chimes gave a brief nod.

"You should have told us," Lei said. You could have been excused from this detail."

"It's fine. Hopefully I can help this go more smoothly. We were classmates at Kamehameha. Class of '83."

"Then let me take the lead," Lei said. "And if it comes to that, you can be 'good cop.'" That was Lei's version of a joke, because she never played anything but bad cop. Sophie smiled.

The house was accessed through a pair of tall, carved tiki columns marking the gate. Chimes spoke into the intercom. "Honolulu Police Department, here on a private matter."

The black wrought iron gate retracted and they drove forward toward a low, plantation-style mansion sprawling over an area of verdant gardens with a stream winding through it and several artificial waterfalls. As Sophie got out of the police SUV, she heard nothing but the call of birds and the trickling of running water.

"Nice place," Lei said. Chimes nodded.

They walked up a wide porch done in lava stone, and Lei

rang the doorbell. A gong echoed somewhere deep inside the house.

A few minutes later, a petite Filipina woman answered the door. She wore black yoga pants and a tank top with a ruffled white apron over the whole outfit. "How can I help you?"

Lei and the sergeant held up their credential wallets, and Sophie held up her ID from Security Solutions. "We are here to search the premises. Here is a warrant," Lei said, handing the document to the housekeeper. "Is Mr. Blackthorne available? We would like to speak to him."

The maid's eyes widened as she took the proffered document. "Wait right here. I will get him." She closed the door with a bang.

Chimes shifted his weight nervously as Lei stood, relaxed but assertive, her hands on her hips and legs slightly spread. Sophie took a moment to check her phone.

A text from Jake: *"What the hell is going on? You were going to call."*

Sophie suppressed irritation and shoved the phone into the back pocket of her black cargo pants as the door opened again.

Brock Blackthorne was five foot eleven inches, and had what Sophie thought of as 'gym muscles'—overdeveloped arms attempting to compensate for a round gut and bandy legs revealed by a pair of baggy golf shorts. Salt-and-pepper hair topped a florid face, and his hazel eyes snapped with intelligence. He held the warrant aloft, his gaze immediately going to Chimes. "Henry. What the hell is this?"

"Hey, Brock." Chimes stepped forward, extending a hand. "Sorry this is coming out of left field. Let me explain."

Blackthorne ignored his gesture. "I've already called my lawyer. What is this about?"

"Sergeant Lei Texeira." Lei stepped forward and held up her

ID. "That is certainly your right. However, we do not have to wait until your attorney arrives to begin our search." She indicated Sophie, who also held up her creds. "Security specialist Sophie Ang will be assisting us with this examination of your home and computers."

Blackthorne's brows snapped together as he held out his hand for their IDs, and with a contemptuous stare, took Chimes's as well. He took a long moment to inspect them, then stood aside from the doorway silently. "My attorney has advised me to cooperate and wait on his arrival."

"Thank you." Lei stepped across the threshold first, followed by a chastened Chimes, with Sophie bringing up the rear.

The interior of the house had a feel of old-world Hawaii charm, with wide-planked polished wood floors that smelled of beeswax and lemon, a collection of gleaming calabashes on a sideboard, and finely woven lauhala matting defining a huge living area decorated in the heavy, curved rattan chairs and couches covered in aloha print that had been popular in the fifties—but the fabric was bright and sturdy, and the rattan gleamed.

Sophie took the latex gloves and handful of evidence bags that Lei handed her, trying to ignore the baleful stare she could feel on her back from their reluctant host.

Chimes approached Blackthorne again. "Hey, man. I'm sorry about this."

"Screw you, Chimes." Blackthorne's voice dripped with contempt.

"Sergeant, why don't you take the kitchen and living room and dining area?" Lei said. Sophie guessed she was trying to defuse the confrontation and remind Chimes of his responsibilities, while giving him a less sensitive zone of the house to search. "Mr. Blackthorne, can you and your staff wait outside, please?"

Thin-lipped, Blackthorne stepped out onto the porch with the maid. Lei continued to direct. "I'll take the bedrooms and bathrooms, and Sophie, you take everything else."

Sophie nodded, heading down a hallway past the den, where Chimes had begun to busy himself pulling books off of a shelf.

What were they looking for? She had to consciously remember: the GPR report for the Kakela site, any artifacts that looked like they might have come from the site, or anything tying Blackthorne to the Hui and/or Mano.

The man's office, or one of the bedrooms possibly, seemed like the most likely area to find any evidence.

Sophie passed several openings off the hall: a guestroom suite, a spacious laundry room, with a small wall-mounted TV playing a Filipino soap opera, a home gym. Finally, at the end of the hall, a closed door.

She turned the handle—it was unlocked.

Blackthorne's office was a beautiful, manly sanctuary. Tall, sliding glass windows framed a stunning view of the mountains beyond the deck outside, a rain squall blowing a transparent blue veil across their heights. Shelves lined with books filled the walls, and a quick scan of titles revealed interests in astrophysics, crime mysteries, and Hawaiiana. Blackthorne's desk was a koa wood monolith, almost buried under stacks of papers held down by a collection of stone poi pounders. His computer beckoned, and Sophie slid her backpack off and set it on his leather office chair.

"It's going to take a while to search this place, so I might as well begin cloning," she muttered, removing the write blocker from her backpack and plugging it in.

It wasn't even necessary to unlock the computer to copy its entire contents to the external drive—but she couldn't wait to see what was on his files.

That task begun, Sophie surveyed the room from the desk's vantage point.

Several major art pieces—impressionistic seascapes—decorated the walls. A couple of club chairs framed a Tiffany standing lamp in colorful stained glass. Sophie imagined curling up in a chair with one of the interesting books from the shelf.

"Back on task." She began opening the drawers, stirring the contents as she sifted through. Pens, paper clips, rubber bands. Signature, date, and address stamps. Embossed stationery, a stack of legal pads. A photo of a woman, a pretty brunette, in a closed black frame. *Girlfriend?* Blackthorne wasn't married.

The large bottom file drawer was locked. Sophie unbent a paper clip, inserted it into the lock, and jiggled until the drawer's simple mechanism gave.

"Aha." Sophie smiled as she pulled up a file labeled *Kakela.*

The file was jammed with newspaper cuttings about the site, topographical maps like she had seen in the Hui's offices, and some handwritten notes.

Sophie set the file aside, already hearing the voice of a defense attorney in her mind: *"There is nothing incriminating here. Blackthorne Industries recently made an offer on the site to restore it privately. Mr. Blackthorne has an interest in Hawaiiana and was doing his homework on a potential investment property."*

What she needed to do was find out what the connection between Mano and Blackthorne was…and that was likely going to be contained in the computer she was going to have to bring in.

She was rifling through more files when Lei walked in, brown curls frizzing out of her ponytail, Chimes bringing up the rear, "We haven't found anything in the personal areas. You?"

"It's going slow. There are some interesting things here. I

haven't had a chance to get past the desk," Sophie said. "Blackthorne seems like the kind to have a safe. I suspect one to be behind one of these bookshelves or a piece of art."

"Yeah, I've searched this kind of office before. Guys like this like to keep their secret stuff secret," Lei said. "Chimes, let's do it. All the books off the shelves, and shake them out."

"He's not going to like that," Chimes groaned, but the two got started.

Sophie stacked any files that looked promising and checked the write blocker—only a third finished. "I have to take this computer in with us. I was hoping to clone it in the time we were here, but you two are going much faster than I am."

"No, you'll have to take it in and look through it in all of your spare time," Lei said. She paused, a hand held aloft as she removed a large seascape. "Bingo." On the wall behind the art was the recessed outline of a safe. "Chimes, get Blackthorne in here to open this for us, or tell him he will have to pay for one of our locksmiths to do it."

Chimes hunched his shoulders miserably, but walked out.

Lei glanced at Sophie. "Getting any gut feelings?"

"My gut feeling is telling me he's involved. There's some connection between these two men—we just have to find out what it was."

"Agree." Lei set the painting down on the floor as Chimes reappeared outside of the office via the porch with Blackthorne in tow, followed by a short Chinese man wearing a tan business suit that reminded Sophie of turn-of-the-century safari garb.

"Perry Chan, Esquire," the attorney said. "I have looked over the warrant, and it does not mention the contents of safes."

"That is implied in the phrase, "thorough search of home and grounds," Lei said, facing the diminutive Chinese man. "Mr. Blackthorne can either open the safe, or my associates and I will remove it from the wall and take it to the station, which I imagine will be a messy and expensive business—for him."

Sophie was glad of the blank expression she'd learned to don to face any threat. She came to stand behind Lei, folding her arms in a pose that pumped up her toned arms.

A long staredown ensued, and it was Blackthorne who broke first. "Nothing in there to see anyway. It's the principle of the thing." He walked up to the safe and took out his wallet, consulting a card and working the combination. He opened the door. "I prefer not to watch you rifle through my personal things. Chan, you make sure they don't take anything." Blackthorne turned and left through the slider onto the porch.

"Chimes, since you have a personal relationship with the witness, why don't you do another sweep for any areas we missed," Lei said.

Chimes ducked his head in assent and left, heading into the house's interior.

Lei reached into the safe and took out a stack of rubber-banded cash, rifling through it, setting it on the desk. Several jewelry sets followed, in black leatherette cases—probably family heirlooms. And finally, a tray of exquisitely carved ivory netsukes, tiny hand-carved Japanese sculptures used to secure sashes and garments in the Japan of ancient times.

The women bent over them, and saw why Blackthorne didn't want to be embarrassed by their examination: they were exquisitely wrought erotica, a plethora of positions, some of which Sophie hadn't known existed.

"Well, I doubt these have anything to do with your case," Chan said, removing the tray and setting it on the desk. "Anything else?"

Lei got up on her tiptoes to peer inside. "No. Empty."

They carefully replaced the items and closed the safe. "We

just need to finish the bookshelves," Lei said. "You can stay or go, Mr. Chan."

"I'll stay, thank you."

Lei and Sophie returned to the shelves, removing the books, shaking them out, replacing them.

Finally, the job was done. "I have to take this computer in," Sophie said, pulling the plug on the device. "And any others Mr. Blackthorne has."

"He has a laptop. He left it in the kitchen on the island."

"Thank you." Sophie preceded Lei back down the hall, and Lei collected the laptop. They opened the front door to find Chimes and Blackthorne faced off.

"You need to tell them what you know about Mano," Chimes said.

"I don't need to do shit," Blackthorne retorted. "Now, I've cooperated. Get the hell off my property."

"Not yet." Chimes firmed his jaw and turned to the women. "Mano was a classmate of ours. I heard rumors about his illegal activities—and I know for a fact that Brock has done several business deals with him. Brock, tell them."

"Mr. Blackthorne doesn't have to tell them any such thing," Chan piped up, approaching from the back exit of the office.

"I think we should have a more formal interview down at the station," Lei said.

Sophie, her arms full of computer equipment, stepped past Blackthorne and headed for the SUV.

She stowed the computer and returned, taking the laptop from Lei, who was now actively arguing with Chan about Blackthorne coming in to the station. "Going to do one more sweep while you discuss this," she said, and headed back into the house.

The maid was replacing the books more neatly into the den's shelves as she passed, and gave Sophie a glare.

Sophie headed back to the office and stood in the doorway, hands on her hips. Something was bothering her visually about the space; she couldn't pinpoint what, but it was something about the design of the room.

The symmetry was off on the right side of the room by about three feet.

Perhaps it was just a closet in the other room, but Sophie's experience with a personal "safe room" in her past had honed her attentiveness to architectural oddities.

She went back out into the hall and looked into the guest suite, frowning.

The same asymmetrical look, a shortening of the room on the left side, mirrored the change in the other room, and it wasn't explained by a closet—the closet was on the right.

Sophie went back into the office and stood, staring at the wall of shelves broken up by a couple of niches for art.

"What are you doing?" Lei said impatiently. "I don't have enough to arrest Blackthorne and make him come in, and Chan is stalling by insisting we do it tomorrow. You up and disappeared on me."

"There's something off with the dimensions of these two rooms," Sophie said. "I think there's a hidden space here."

"I'll get Blackthorne." Lei spun on her heel. "That bastard isn't telling us everything."

"No, I'm not." Blackthorne's gravelly voice came from the glass sliders, and both women spun toward him, hands dropping to their weapons. "You two look like a couple of Bond girls, all ready to shoot me." His voice dripped sarcasm.

"Where is this secret room?" Lei barked. "We are entitled to search any and all areas of the house and grounds."

"That doesn't mean I have to disclose them." Blackthorne's ill humor continued even though he had won the skirmish over going into the station. "But it appears you want to see my wine cellar."

Blackthorne walked over to the wall of shelves and depressed a hidden button. A section of shelving popped out with a soft *ping*. A draft of cool air lifted the tiny hairs on Sophie's neck and she peered into the dark, able to discern shelves lining the narrow space. The light gleamed on hundreds of wine bottles lying on their sides at a slant.

"I keep rare vintages in here. This wine room is climate controlled. Some of these bottles are worth thousands." Blackthorne gestured to Sophie. "There's only room for one at a time to go in. Since you discovered my secret, perhaps you would like to go in first?"

She would rather not go in first, at all.

Sophie felt the tightness of old fear constrict her lungs and loosen the joints of her legs, making her feel wobbly and out of breath. Darkness and small spaces had become necessary for sleeping, but that was an adaptation to her marital imprisonment and abuse—not something she wanted forced upon her in a strange house by a suspect. Lei read her expression and frowned, stepping forward. "I'll go."

"No, it's fine." Sophie brushed past Blackthorne and stepped into the cool, musty-smelling darkness, her shoulder brushing one of the racks of wine bottles.

A sensor light bloomed into brightness dead ahead, illuminating a wooden stairway between the shelves, leading down into darkness. Sophie barely had time to register that when she felt a rough, hard shove, and flew forward down the steps.

Sophie's arms flew out instinctively, seeking some way to break her fall. Her fingers caught on a wooden balustrade, and she curled them desperately, her body swinging around to plummet into the wall of wine bottles lining the stairway.

The door she'd entered through shut with a bang above her as she lost her grip, tumbling down to crash into a black metal door at the base of the stairs.

Sophie tried to get to her feet, pain screaming at her from her knees, side, elbows, and wrist, but when she tried to stand, her ankle collapsed and a shaft of agony shot up her leg and wrenched a cry from her lips.

Blackthorne grabbed her by the back of the head, his fingers knotting in her thick hair, and smashed her head into the door.

A burst of colored light. Then nothing.

Chapter 17

Sophie was lying on her stomach on the floor, her face turned to the side, and that was all she knew for certain.

As her hearing booted up, she heard muttering. The muttering came from her right, and it was Blackthorne's dark rasp of a voice. "This is it. It all comes down to this. It all was leading to this, and it will all end here."

Sophie stayed perfectly still, her breathing gentle and even, her eyes closed. A dim red glow against her eyelids told her of a nearby light source.

She assessed herself for injuries. The ankle was bad, at least sprained. Her forehead was already swelling into a knot, and tingly numbness spread down her cheeks, along with pulses of pain. Possible brain trauma, indicated by the fact that her body did not want to obey when she told it to move.

More bruises screamed at her. Her knee was wrenched, her hip bruised, her hands throbbed.

But that was not her biggest problem. The biggest problem was pacing back and forth in front of that light source, causing moving black shadows across her closed eyes.

Far away, she heard pounding.

Lei was trying to get in, trying to get to her, trying to rescue her.

What was going on with Blackthorne? There must be evidence down here that would link him to the murder…nothing else made sense to explain his irrational action.

Sophie's thoughts were sluggish, bubbling up from somewhere inside her injured brain, trying to form into substance but flickering past her consciousness before she could capture them.

The longer he thought she was knocked out, the better able she would be to respond to whatever came next.

She clung to that idea, capturing it, keeping it in a spot between her eyebrows.

Nearby, a cell phone rang with an incongruously cheerful electronic melody.

"You can't get me out of here until I am ready to leave," Blackthorne said. "Ang is alive, but she won't be if you continue trying to get in here. This is an internal safe room, with bomb shelter walls. It cannot be breached without serious effort, and I will hear you coming and kill her."

A chill rippled across Sophie, raising the hairs on her arms at the certainty in Blackthorne's voice. Sophie was in trouble. Deep trouble.

This man was unbalanced. And she was his hostage, locked in with him in a steel basement.

Tendrils of panic curled through Sophie, brushing along her nerves and tightening her belly, speeding her heartbeat. Assan Ang had locked her in a room not much different from this one.

But this was not that situation.

And, even if it had a few similarities, she had escaped Assan, a deadly sadist. She could escape Blackthorne, too.

An unwelcome memory bubbled up: Assan was free again.

Sophie kept her breathing calm with an effort. Blackthorne ended the call, and began the muttering and pacing again.

How could they have been so wrong about him? He had seemed every inch the successful businessman, but clearly something deeper was going on. *Something involving Mano.*

Maybe she could get him talking. Build a bond with him. That's what they had told her in her FBI training on hostage negotiation, seemingly a hundred years ago.

Sophie needed to seem cowed, helpless. She needed to appeal to Blackthorne's vanity and exploit any bond she could make with him. He had not asked Lei for any demands, which told her they would be here for a while as the negotiation process unfolded.

Sophie just needed to stay calm and alert, and appeal to his masculinity.

If only that weren't one of the things she was terrible at, and her head was not so sore. But Assan had taught her well, and now she needed to remember those lessons.

She gave a low moan, not much of a performance considering the pain.

Immediately, Blackthorne leaned over her. He blocked the red source of light, and she could feel his stale breath on her face. "Don't move. I have you covered.

Sophie moaned again. "I have no intention of going anywhere. I think my ankle is sprained, and I have a concussion at least."

"Still. Precautions are in order." Blackthorne wrenched her arms up behind her back, whipping some sort of rope around her wrists.

Sophie turned her head to the side and emitted a loud, theatrical groan, lacing her fingers together and bracing her palms apart to get some distance as he bound her. "Please. Not so tight."

The old law enforcement trick worked, and she had some

wiggle room in the bonds as he finished the lashing. He moved her legs, and Sophie didn't have to fake the sharp cry of anguish as he touched her injured ankle. "Please! Please, I'm not going anywhere with my ankle like this."

Blackthorne's hands hesitated on her throbbing ankle.

This was not a man who was used to hurting others.

Blackthorne was trapped in an escalating situation.

The thoughts, as if being read aloud by her hostage negotiation instructor, unspooled across her consciousness. *"Always assess the psychology of the hostage taker,"* her instructor would have said. *"Once you understand his or her emotional motivation, you hold the key to what will de-escalate the situation."*

Blackthorne was what he appeared, for the most part. Now he was driven by desperation—there was something incriminating in the room that she'd been about to find, and he was going to get busted for the Mano murder. She had to give him hope, and a sense of control.

Blackthorne walked away without binding her feet, and she could feel regret and disgust in his heavy footsteps as he began his pacing again.

He did not want to hurt her, and that was to her advantage.

"Thank you," she whispered. "I won't do anything. I want to live."

Blackthorne snorted. "Of course you do. You'll say anything to live. We all want to live. Some of us want to live forever."

Was this his pathology? Did he have some obsession with death, immortality, making history…anything that she could exploit?

Sophie wished she was feeling more acute, that she understood human psychology better, and as she often did, she wished she had Marcella's grasp of human nature and gift for flattery—or even Lei's quick, dogged way of manipulating witnesses in an interview.

But Sophie was herself, brilliant in some ways, and limited in others. At least she knew what those ways were. "Can you help me sit up? I want to know about living forever."

A long beat went by. Sophie practically held her breath, and then he was behind her, lifting her under her arms, dragging her to a surprisingly soft armchair, the last thing she would have expected in a safe room like this.

Sophie opened her eyes at last as Blackthorne tucked a pillow behind her upper back so that she wasn't leaning against her bound wrists.

More evidence that he wanted her to be comfortable, that he didn't want to hurt or kill her.

She looked up at his square, flushed face. She fluttered her eyelashes, as if overcome by fear and some other emotion. "Thank you."

Blackthorne moved away and resumed his pacing. Upright, her head really swam, and she leaned it against the chair's padded, high back. Sudden nausea at the change of position swamped her, and Sophie heaved forward and vomited, her stomach knotting, her body contorting.

"Son of a bitch!" Blackthorne lifted her out of the chair and laid her on her side on the floor in front of it. He put the pillow under her head. She had brought up nothing but bile, but now the room smelled sharply foul.

"Glad you didn't have much in there, but it still reeks."

"I'm sorry. So sorry." Sophie let tears creep into her voice— again, it wasn't hard. She was in agony, and the symptoms of head injury were not something she was faking. She shut her eyes and rested a moment as Blackthorne began his muttering again, walking over to a large metal cabinet in one corner of the room, and retrieving a roll of paper towels and a spray bottle of disinfectant. He scrubbed up Sophie's vomit, grimacing as he did so, muttering under his breath.

He was muttering in Hawaiian. Sophie spoke four languages, but Hawaiian was not one of them.

"Tell me what you want," Sophie said. "I used to be an FBI agent. I am trained in situations like this. I know what they will do. And I can help us get out."

Blackthorne had hazel eyes that hinted at the mixed Hawaiian heritage he must have had to have qualified for attendance at Kamehameha School. The expression in those eyes was hard as river stone as he looked at her now. "I don't think you can help. And I don't want to hear your voice anymore."

So much for building a bond.

Sophie nodded and shut her eyes, marshaling her resources. She was able to wriggle her wrists within the restraints, and the circulation cut off was not too bad, considering. She tried to work them apart, but the skin of her wrists quickly chafed.

What could she do to help herself now?

Keep him talking. Appeal to his vanity.

She looked around the room, and saw rows of shelving, lined with small black collector's boxes. Artifacts were mounted in square, lit display cases: and the subject of his collecting was readily apparent.

Blackthorne collected Hawaiiana.

Sophie's mind started clicking at last. There must be a connection, more than just blackmail, between Blackthorne and Mano. She'd put money on the probability of Mano selling the GPR report to Blackthorne before he was killed.

She just needed to find out what that connection was, what Blackthorne had been after at the site—*and whether or not he had found it.*

At the very least, it would fill the time.

As if in response to her thoughts, Blackthorne's phone begin to buzz and jump with an incoming call. Blackthorne stared at it malevolently, hands on his hips.

"You should give them a demand to work on," Sophie said. "If you don't, they'll just keep calling. They may assume I'm already dead, and mount an assault to break in. Consider giving them proof of life by letting me speak to them. That will buy you more time to figure out what you want to do."

Blackthorne spun to face her, his face darkly congested with rage, and she wondered how she had so misread this businessman with his golf belly and muscle arms.

"People underestimate you all the time, don't they?" Sophie said.

"Yes, they do. And I will show them all who I really am." For the first time, Blackthorne's expression softened slightly as he gazed at her. "I'm sorry for this. You're just collateral damage."

This was not good. Blackthorne had made up his mind about the outcome of the standoff.

But maybe she could still make it out alive, even if he chose not to.

Blackthorne advanced to the same cabinet where he had procured the cleaning supplies, and this time he took out a magnificent red and yellow feather shoulder cape, in a classic pattern she recognized from her trip to the Bishop Museum. The cape was covered in a transparent, breathable fabric cover with a zipper. He extracted the garment reverently and laid it over the back of the club chair she had recently vacated. He stroked the bright feathers, thousands of bits of plumage from tiny native birds, with his fingertips.

"Tell me about your collection," she said softly. *Keep him talking. Flatter him. Learn what you can. Get him to like you.*

He returned to the cabinet and removed a tapa cloth *malo,* a loincloth made of finely pounded mulberry bark stamped with tribal patterns in natural inks. Sophie could tell that this piece of fabric was a reproduction by its newness.

His back turned to her, Blackthorne took off his clothing down to a pair of white cotton Hanes underwear, the kind of odd juxtaposition that, like the silly song of his ringtone, was the only reminder that they were not in a place out of time.

This was not going well. Either SWAT would break in and they would die then, or he would simply kill her whenever he was finished with the ritual he was creating.

"You are right about people underestimating me. I am sick of being taken for nothing but a *haole."* Blackthorne's voice vibrated with suppressed passion. "I can trace my lineage all the way through the line of Kamehameha III, the greatest king of Hawaii."

"That must be why you wanted to purchase the Kakela site, his former royal palace," Sophie said.

Blackthorne did not respond. He draped and knotted the *malo* around his waist and between his legs. Finally getting it the way he wanted it, he turned to face her. She was surprised by the elaborate pattern of Polynesian tattoo designs crisscrossing his chest and abdomen.

"Tell me everything about your collection. Tell me what you wanted with Kakela."

"I told you to stop talking." Blackthorne removed a folding knife from the cabinet, and cut off one of the sleeves of his business shirt. Walking over to Sophie, he twisted her head to the side and gagged her with the sleeve, tightening a knot in the cloth at the back of her head.

The material instantly dried her tongue and stretched her cheeks, and Sophie swallowed with difficulty, her jaw ajar. A sense of hopelessness and futility swamped her. Familiar darkness rose behind her eyes, and she closed them.

There was no sense struggling anymore. What would be, would be. *But if she got any opportunity to escape, she would take it.* She was a fighter. A survivor.

Right now, she didn't feel like one.

Blackthorne finished his preparations by scooping a handful of hardened coconut oil from a small calabash into his palms, rubbing them together, and anointing his body.

"I am the reincarnation of Kamehameha III," he said.

Whatever Sophie had expected him to say, this was not it. Her eyes popped open wide.

"I became aware of this through channeling the *mana* of my ancestors through my collection of bone hooks. They recognized me and told me who I was."

Keep him talking. Be his witness. Sophie nodded her head, trying to convey with her eyes an encouraging feeling for him to go on, but even that slight movement made nausea roil through her belly, and she worried, that, with the gag in her mouth, she could choke.

"Would you like to see my collection? They will all go to the Bishop Museum. I only borrowed them, anyway. They belong to all of our people."

He sounded so sane. She blinked hard to convey a *yes.*

Blackthorne walked over to a tall, black steel cabinet and opened it. Inside, shallow shelves of trays lined the cabinet from top to bottom. He removed the top tray and carried it over, kneeling beside Sophie so that she could see the collection.

Each bone hook was nested in a niche of black velvet. The sacred objects seemed to glow with a patina of age and power. Their color ranged from a soft ivory white to a deep, tea-colored stain. Sophie recognized various styles from her brief overview at the Bishop. Blackthorne removed a large, beautifully carved decorative hook from the center of the collection. He held it on his palm and extended it for her to see. "This hook is made from the bones of my queen," he said. "It's new."

Sophie just stared. *New? What did that mean?*

"I tried to buy the Kakela site so that she could be restored and returned to her rest, protected and memorialized properly. But they refused my offer, so she will have to remain here with us."

Sophie blinked her eyes to show that she understood. He had found what he was seeking. *He had to have had the GPR report to find the queen's burial site in the buried canoe.*

Blackthorne nodded as if she had agreed, and went on. "I worry that when they breach this place, they will not understand the importance of these hooks. They will not know who they belong to, where they were obtained. I will spend some of the time remaining to us providing documentation."

So he was planning for the breach.

Dread curdled Sophie's stomach—so much could go wrong with a breach, and Blackthorne was armed and only semi-rational. But he was showing her his collection—he must mean for her to be a witness?

Sophie blinked and he nodded, as if they were having a conversation. Blackthorne straightened up, and left the hooks beside Sophie. "You just rest. Feel the *mana* of my ancestors."

Blackthorne walked over to the armchair and donned the feather cape with a flourish. As he looked at her, in his tattoos and ancient garb, Sophie could almost see why he thought he was the greatest Hawaiian king, returned in the flesh. There was something timeless in his bearing and this moment.

But he was going to kill her, and himself. She wished he would let her speak so she could ask him what was the point of being a reincarnation if he was killed? But he would probably just say that he would come back again.

She closed her eyes, and just rested, hearing nothing but the faint rustle of a pen and paper.

What was Lei doing? It was likely that her team was planning an assault. They might begin by trying to make the space uncomfortable, trying to manipulate the temperature, or even cutting off the air supply. Anything to move Blackthorne toward some conclusion of the standoff. And without proof of life, the team might well assume that Sophie was already dead.

But she certainly hoped not. Perhaps by being passive, she could get Blackthorne to lose interest in her.

Blackthorne finally straightened up. He returned, and crouched down beside her with a series of plain white labels that had been marked with a location and date. "I have a database set up on my computer, but you have my computer." He looked up with a faint smile, and she blinked again, opening her eyes wide to show her interest. He smiled again, both sad and a little ironic, a closed-mouth tug of the lips that somehow conveyed those nuances to Sophie.

It was as if Sophie's helplessness and silence freed him.

Maybe he was a little more like Assan Ang than she had originally thought.

He arranged the bone hooks in a circle on the floor, carefully setting the correct label beneath each one.

"My Hawaiian ancestors were warlike, contrary to popular belief. They practiced human sacrifice, and they believed in the transfer of *mana* from one person to another. If I'm going to come back again after this, I will need help."

Sophie shut her eyes and swallowed around the gag, the hope that had begun to bloom dying. He meant to kill her, after all. *Collateral damage.* A human sacrifice.

If only her head didn't hurt so badly. If only her ankle wasn't sprained. But it was, and if she was going to survive this, she had to defeat him. There was no other choice. There was no rescue coming through that locked door.

Blackthorne went on. "I've turned on a recorder so that posterity can know what went on here. What I tried to do. Who I was." With dim light gleaming on his oiled tattoos, he looked every inch the returned king—except for his white skin and bald spot.

Again, so many juxtapositions.

Sophie wiggled her feet, trying to get circulation going. The one advantage she had managed to wring from him was keeping her feet free. Her hands, too, while firmly bound, had a little wiggle room. Maybe she could get one of them out.

"Mano did not understand what this was about for me. We were classmates at Kamehameha, and he always knew I was special. Different. But he didn't respect it. He thought it was because of my missionary name. But that's not the part of me that is mighty, that will be remembered forever."

Sophie couldn't believe it, but she was gaining an inch in wiggling her hands out of the bindings, and having made up her mind that she had to kill him first, it seemed as if strength was pouring into her body, greater strength than a mere adrenaline hit.

The headache was gone and Sophie focused her eyes on Blackthorne's back as she worked her hands against the ropes while he meticulously rearranged the bone hooks in their large circle on the floor. He rose to his feet and returned to the cabinet, pulling out the deepest drawer at the bottom.

Sophie continued her frantic working at the bindings. Her skin gave way, and the slickness of blood began to lubricate the ropes. She didn't even feel it.

Blackthorne turned back and carried the large, heavy drawer over to the edge of the circle closest to Sophie. "I want you to see this." He approached her and that was the cue to stop her relentless working at the ropes. Blackthorne lifted her shoulders and dragged her closer to the circle. Grasping her short, thick, curly hair, he held her head aloft to look into the 4' x 1' box shelf.

Sophie gave a gasp, muffled by the gag, and her head swam nauseously as she glimpsed the contents of the tray: a skeleton, the bones stained the rust red of Lahaina soil, gleaming in the overhead light.

"My wife. My queen." Blackthorne stroked the dome of the skull reverently. "She has been lost to me all this time, and in this life, I have been looking for her. But we will have another time."

Sophie shivered, ripples of fear chasing over her skin. *Blackthorne was unhinged.*

Blackthorne released her head, patting her hair gently. "For some reason I keep thinking of that quote from Jefferson: 'from time to time, the tree of liberty must be refreshed by the blood of patriots and tyrants.' I don't know if it completely applies here, but the tree of our power must be watered by the blood of someone brave, someone with plenty of her own *mana*. And you certainly have that."

He turned around and began taking the bones out of the tray, caressing each one in a sensual way as he interspersed them between the bone hooks.

Sophie resumed her abrading of the ropes, focusing on sliding her right hand up and down. The blood slicking the rope was softening it. Must be some kind of hemp, not a synthetic rope, one part of her mind remotely observed. The strength that continued to surge through her in life-giving pulses cleared her foggy brain and erased the throb of her ankle.

There was *mana* in the room all right, and it was helping her.

Pounding began on the exterior of the steel door, muffled by some sort of soundproofing. Blackthorne's head flew up, and his eyes narrowed. "We don't have much time."

No, Sophie didn't. She tightened her abs, drawing her knees up against her chest, curling her back to give herself more room. As Blackthorne went back to his preparations, turning his back to her, she dug deep and, using core strength and her shoulder for leverage, she rolled up onto her knees. He heard the movement and swiveled to look at her.

She kept her eyes down, her position on her knees mutely submissive.

This had been one of Assan's favorite positions for her: meeting him at the door when he came home from work, on her knees, with a restraint ready for his pleasure, her head bent and eyes down.

Blackthorne gave her a long look before he turned away and finished setting out the bones. He rose to his feet, his back to her, clearly satisfied that she was merely awaiting his performance. He walked back to the cabinet as the pounding changed to the high-pitched whine of a drill.

"Perhaps you were right. I should have given them a demand to work on. They obviously don't value your life."

Sophie had her right hand halfway out of the bindings. The rope was caught on one of the tiny bones in the back of her hand, and there was no help for it. She gave a massive tug with her biceps and the tiny bone snapped, a reverberation through her body that still did not translate into pain.

Something, or someone, was helping her.

Thank you, God, and mana of the ancestors.

She shook the binding off her bleeding, broken hand, but kept both of them behind her back in the same submissive position.

Blackthorne had underestimated her, and he wouldn't have a chance to again.

Chapter 18

The king brushed the feathers of his 'ahu 'ula cape—so soft, so rare. It was amazing that the vivid color of the multitude of tiny 'I'iwi and O'o feathers had lasted so long.

The whine of the drill from the team breaking in from outside was getting louder—they were going after a couple of places on the door to guess by the different pitches of the tools.

He straightened to look down at the bone circle on the floor of the safe room.

Such beauty: his hooks drew in the mana, and the bones of his queen focused it.

He glanced back at the woman. She gazed at him, her head down but her eyes pleading from her position on her knees.

She must think he was going to have mercy on her, but he could not. His return demanded a release of more mana, a flow of blood to strengthen his journey. Still, she was an appealing sight. She had caramel skin, huge dark eyes, and a truly lovely face though marred by a terrible scar across one cheekbone and up into her dense, curly hair. Somehow the scar made her more interesting.

He wished he could leave her alive, but a king never flinched from what needed to be done.

He walked over to the cabinet and removed the ceremonial knife. He had not been able to find a Hawaiian one; this was a lesser tool, but would have to do, and at least was not something as crude as the metal pocketknife he'd used earlier.

He turned to face her, the obsidian weapon, knapped by a Native American several hundred years ago, balanced across his palms.

He didn't want a big, messy scene. She was strong, and even with her bindings, would thrash about and disturb his arrangements. Better to lure her inside the circle, trick her into submitting.

"Some blood must be spilled to release more mana. I am going to make a small incision in my leg into the circle," he said, approaching her. "You have some medical training. Show me a place that will be safe for the first aid team to treat when they get in here. I'm going to move you inside the circle so you can show me the right place to do it."

Hope bloomed in her eyes, and she nodded. He liked her gagged and silent—that was how women should be. The women he paid to have sex with in Chinatown loved being tied and gagged.

Pain tightened the lines of her body as she lowered her head and closed her eyes trustingly at his approach. Her ankle, tucked beneath her, was hugely swollen.

Poor thing. Her suffering would be over soon.

He tucked the obsidian knife into his malo as he approached her, grasping her under the arms to lift her as he'd done before—but this time, her arms flew open and grabbed him by the ankles, so fast he hardly had time to register what was happening.

The woman surged to her feet with a howl muffled by the gag, her strength unbelievable as she yanked him right off his feet. He crashed down into the circle, his head bouncing off the concrete floor.

Stars filled his vision and he tried to roll onto his side, but she came down on him, her elbow stabbing him in the gut, blowing out his air. She flipped him onto his stomach and leapt on his back. He writhed beneath her with all his strength, just trying to get a breath, as she whipped the knife out of his malo and pulled his head back by his hair.

He went utterly still, feeling the jagged, razor sharp edge of the knife at his throat, her inarticulate, muffled growls of rage in his ear.

"Do it," he whispered. "Send me back to my ancestors."

Another long moment. He felt her strength, her restraint—and her indecision. He shut his eyes, waiting, then yelled, "Do it!"

The door came down behind them with a ground-shaking crash.

He was out of time. "Kill me!" he screamed.

Still she hesitated. He could feel her looking back over her shoulder at the SWAT team, hear their thumping boots.

The king wrenched his hair out of her hand and flung his head forward and his throat onto the blade.

It didn't hurt.

He had thought it would hurt as his blood spurted. It didn't, but his lungs burned and bubbled, his vision dimmed, and his body twitched, losing motor control as she flopped him onto his back and pressed the loose part of the feather cape against the wound in his neck, screaming for help through her gag.

She was ruining the feathers of his precious cape. When he came back in the next life, he would find her and punish her for that.

Chapter 19

The medics must have been right behind SWAT, because two of them pulled Sophie off of Blackthorne, and immediately went to work trying to stanch the wound in his neck. She staggered, gasping for breath against the gag as two SWAT team members caught Sophie under the arms. A knife flashed and the gag was gone, and she groaned at the sensation of at last being able to close her aching mouth.

"I didn't kill him," she said. "He lunged onto the blade. I was restraining him." Trembling and thin, her voice sounded like it came from somewhere far away, and the SWAT officer holding the arm with the broken hand pushed the black, anonymous-looking helmet up to reveal a familiar face. "Lei," Sophie whispered, relief at seeing her friend's warm brown eyes weakening her knees.

"Damn, girl," Lei said. "Trust you to take down the perp when we thought you might be dead." She hugged Sophie, pressing her close, and inadvertently jarred her hand. Sophie yelped, pulling her broken hand up against her chest as her head swam and her knees buckled.

Whatever the force had been that had given her super strength departed, and Sophie folded like a puppet with cut strings, blackness dropping over her like the curtain at the end of a performance.

* * *

She was moving, jostling, held close in someone's arms. Everything hurt, but especially her head. And her hand. And her ankle...*she was a mess.* This was worse than her big fight with the Punisher last year...

She had gone somewhere for a minute but was back.

Someone was carrying her. Why wasn't she on a gurney? Who was strong enough to carry a five foot nine, hundred and forty-pound woman up a flight of stairs and across that huge house?

Jake Dunn.

She recognized his familiar smell, made acrid with fear and stress and adrenaline.

They had been here before: she injured, him carrying her— and now she recognized his voice, a low rumble in his chest against her ear. He emitted a stream of profanity mixed with prayers, as if he could curse God into getting his way.

"I'm okay." Her voice was muffled but clear. She was proud of that. "Sprained ankle, broken hand, and a concussion, but I'm okay."

Jake stopped. She kept her eyes closed, afraid to see what was in his face as he looked down at her. "Good. We have to stop doing this," he said.

"On that we agree."

They reached the ambulance, and she finally opened her eyes as he settled her on a gurney. Jake's face was a mask of distress looming over her, his gray eyes stormy, as the EMTs strapped her down and barraged her with questions. Sophie ignored them and fixed her gaze on Jake. "Call Todd Remarkian," Sophie said. "Call Todd and tell him to meet me at the hospital. Tell him I need him."

Then Sophie shut her eyes so she didn't have to see how she'd hurt him.

Chapter 20

Sophie spent the night in the hospital for observation but was discharged the next morning, her hand splinted and on crutches for the sprained ankle. Lei walked beside her as Connor pushed her wheelchair out of the hospital toward one of Security Solutions' SUVs.

"I want you to come to my place," Connor said. "There's better security." He had spent the night in a chair by her bedside holding her hand, and she'd been glad of the company.

"No. I want to go to my own place. Mary Watson's," Sophie said.

"Why does she need security?" Lei scrunched her brow. "'Kamehameha III' is safely in the morgue. I am going to have to do an official debrief with you, anyway."

"She needs security because that scumbag Assan Ang is still loose. I don't want her to take any chances," Connor said.

Sophie's brain felt sluggish from the remains of the concussion and pain medication, but she struggled to assess her choices.

Connor's place was out. She was not ready to be alone with him in his home, even for a short time—it felt too much like giving ground, like making a commitment. Calling for him when she was vulnerable was all she felt capable of right now.

Mary Watson's identity and home were secret—*but how secret would her alter ego be with Connor, Marcella, Jake, and Lei all visiting her there?*

"Take me to my father's apartment," she rasped. "They have good security. And Lei—can you pick up my dog? I miss Ginger."

She told her friend where to get Ginger, and sighed as Connor settled her into the buttery leather of the high-end SUV. "Thank you."

He slammed the door harder than necessary.

She glanced over at Connor as he hopped into the driver's seat. His eyes were a brief blaze of turquoise in his stubbled face as they met hers, then he turned on the vehicle, put it in gear, and focused on the road. His linen shirt was crumpled from sleeping in the armchair, and so were his black slacks, and even unshaven and disheveled, he was almost too handsome. "I don't like it."

"You don't have to like it. But thanks for coming and helping me, anyway." She made her voice firm and low.

"I want to put an operative on you. I haven't found Ang since he escaped."

"I'm okay with you putting an operative on me—it's your company, and I'm an employee who's taken a few too many hits lately." Sophie sighed. "I told you that Assan knows how to stay off the grid. And he has a lot of contacts and people who owe him all over the world."

"He must, if I can't find him. I can protect you at my place, though."

"It's not your job to protect me."

"Isn't it?" Again, the brief blaze of his eyes. "I can't lose you now that I found you. *Damn* it."

"No, it isn't your job to protect me. I can protect myself just fine." Stubbornness and pride drove her words. She glanced over at Connor.

His lips were pinched, his jaw tight. He radiated frustration. "These situations you keep getting into are not reassuring me that you have it all together."

"Just ask Blackthorne who won our little standoff yesterday," Sophie said. "Getting injured on the job is part of the risk of my work, as you well know. But I'm not an idiot. I know Assan is a huge threat and not to be underestimated. After what he had done to the last guy I kissed...well, you're in danger too. Because of all of that, I would appreciate it if you'd stay with me at my father's apartment until I get back on my feet."

Connor slanted her a glance that made her toes curl. "You sure about that?"

"I am." She stroked his arm with her good hand, and smiled.

Chapter 21

L ei took Sophie's official statement accompanied by Sergeant Chimes at Sophie's father's elegant penthouse apartment upon their arrival. Dr. Kinoshita, Security Solutions' staff psychologist, came by and did her post-incident psych debrief. Exhausted and headachy by then, Sophie went to bed while Connor fixed her chicken soup, worked his business on her computers, and played with their dogs.

Having Connor in her space was remarkably easy, and made her feel safe. She slept well and ate well, blossoming under his nurturing. Cuddling and kisses heated things up between them, but Connor was a gentleman and she knew he'd wait as long as she needed him to for more—and she wanted to be totally healed so that she could make the most of that moment.

Lei finally called Sophie on the fifth day after the standoff to tell her that the investigation into Mano's murder was concluded. The recording from the interior safe that Blackthorne had made backed up Sophie's videotaped statement of events. "I wish we could find some physical evidence tying Blackthorne to Mano's body, but there was nothing on the body besides that one hair, which doesn't match anything on or around Blackthorne. Still, as the DA pointed out, there are a million ways a body can pick up an anonymous hair, and we're closing the case. His death has officially been ruled a suicide. Blackthorne was certainly off his nut."

"I haven't heard that phrase before, but I can guess its meaning," Sophie said. A shiver rippled down her spine as Connor nibbled a spot behind her ear. "I'm just glad everything is wrapped up."

"Well enough. And the Bishop Museum is very happy to have his collection of bone hooks and the bones of the queen. His estate was left to the museum as well, and they are planning to turn his home into an extension of the museum. There was a surprise in his will, too—a major bequest to benefit the Hui to Restore Kakela. The queen will get her proper resting place, after all."

"I think the ghost of Kamehameha would have liked that," Sophie said.

She ended the call and turned around into Connor's arms, and lost herself in a kiss.

Chapter 22

Sophie got off the plane on Maui a few days later, wearing a neoprene brace and off her crutches. A small, light resin cast on her hand and the last of her laser treatments to remove her scar were completed. She was on the Valley Isle for multiple purposes: to pick up her possessions from the condo that she'd thought she would return to, to drop by the Kakela site to pick up the final check for Security Solutions and remove their battered tech equipment, and to deliver the surprise bequest from Blackthorne's estate to the Hui to restore the queen's burial site. After all of that, she was meeting Jake out at the rock star's house to get started on their next job.

Leaving the recovery cocoon at her father's place had been difficult, but business pressed in on both her and Connor. She planned to assume her Mary Watson identity once the job on Maui was over, and go back to her anonymous little apartment, though neither of them would relax until Assan Ang was back in custody—*or dead.*

Sophie hadn't asked, but was fairly certain the Ghost was working on a plan involving the latter.

The mischievous wind of Maui tugged at Sophie's lengthening curls as she waited on the curb at the Maui Airport for Jake, who'd flown back to the island right after her rescue to resume his work for Shank Miller.

"Howdy, stranger," Jake hollered through the rolled-down window of a shiny black Toyota Tacoma loaded with ocean sports equipment on roof racks—several surfboards, a single man canoe, the colorful foils of rolled kiteboard sails.

Sophie grinned, relief that he wasn't going to make things awkward lifting her voice into buoyant as she opened the passenger door and tossed her backpack into the extended cab. "Trust you, Jake, to make the most of a job and find some ways to play."

"You got that right." Jake tugged down his mirrored sunglasses to peer at her over the rims. "You look...much better. Well-rested."

There was an edge to his voice.

Sophie shrugged, hoping she wasn't blushing. She wasn't ready to joke about her relationship with Connor, especially with Jake. "Just needed a little time to recover. I told you I was okay."

Jake bounced his brows at her suggestively, but said no more as he maneuvered the truck away from the curb. "What's your first stop?"

"I have to go to the Kakela site and take down the tech equipment there. I'd appreciate your help." She waggled her hand. The resin cast was lightweight, and only covered her hand, leaving the wrist mobile, but it was still going to provide challenges in taking down the surveillance equipment strung up around the site.

"I always knew you only wanted me for my body."

Sophie glanced at Jake sharply, but his eyes were on the road ahead, and a smile curved his mouth. *Just more of his borderline inappropriate humor.*

"I also have to meet with Pomai Magnuson to give her a

check from the Blackthorne estate and pick up our billing. I was hoping you could take down the tech equipment while I meet with Pomai in the trailer. She's on her way."

"No problem. I cleared my schedule this morning."

"Thank you. Why don't you tell me what the latest is with the rock star job? How are things coming along at Shank Miller's?"

Jake proceeded to fill her in as they drove along the curving Pali Highway to Lahaina. Sophie sneaked glances past him to take in the vistas, hoping to spot whale spume out off the coast.

"The grounds are mostly secure; I'm interviewing now for his ongoing security team. I was saving you to install the nanny cam A.I. system," he concluded.

"So it appears we will be here on Maui several weeks at least," Sophie said, unable to keep a note of despondency out of her voice. "That software has to learn the host's habit patterns and needs a lot of training and adjustment at first."

"Can't wait to get back to the boyfriend, can you?" This time there was definitely an edge to Jake's tone.

Sophie frowned. *Maybe he was feeling unappreciated.* "I never thanked you for helping me out of Blackthorne's vault when I was injured. How did you even know where I was?"

"Lei kept me apprised, because I asked her to. Knew I couldn't count on you to communicate."

Sophie narrowed her eyes in annoyance. *He wasn't stopping with the verbal jabs.*

Jake went on. "I was already on island for Security Solutions' business when I heard things were going south with your case." He tightened his jaw, and the muscle in his cheek seemed to vibrate. "Second time I've about had a heart attack."

"Well, thanks for the concern—but I don't think it was necessary. There were plenty of people around, and I'm sure the SWAT team and the medics could have gotten me out of there without your help." A flush heated Sophie's neck at the memory of being carried out by Jake—she hadn't even been surprised it was him, and she'd felt safe, comforted—feelings she didn't associate with him on a daily basis. Affection and annoyance were more the usual, with a swirl of sexual attraction, if she were totally honest.

Sophie's frown had begun to feel stitched onto her forehead. She couldn't understand or like her conflicting feelings. Avoidance was definitely the best policy. *She didn't want to think of anyone but Connor.* "I'm not sure this partnership is working. I think I'll ask Bix to reassign me."

A long pause. Sophie glanced over at Jake. His eyes were forward, his hands white-knuckled on the wheel of the truck, but his voice was carefully casual as he said, "I would have appreciated you telling me that before I briefed you on the Miller case. If I'm going to be working with another operative, I could have saved the update so I didn't have to repeat myself."

"Sorry. I will tell Bix I'm just not physically up to working again so soon on an off-island job. He can find something for me back on Oahu and get you another partner."

"And what will you tell him about getting another partner?" Jake truly sounded like he didn't care—curious, a little annoyed. "Because I'm not going to make something up for you. You're the one having a problem."

The beauty of Maui: glittering cobalt ocean, fluffy clouds, swaying palms—all of it passed unseeing by Sophie's eyes. She wished she were anywhere but here. It was hard for her to confront him—his size, loud voice, overbearing manner—it all made her want to retreat after her years with Assan. *But he wasn't Assan.* He would never abuse or mistreat her. And didn't he deserve the truth after all they'd been through together, in such a short time?

"No, Jake, you're the one having a problem. You don't like me being with Todd."

Jake snorted and flapped a hand. "Sleeping with the boss? Sure, go for it. Shack up with the CEO of our company. Way to work your way up."

Sophie's frown deepened. She didn't like his tone and didn't understand all his euphemisms, but the gist came through loud and clear. *And what was his tone?* Sarcasm? Or hurt?

Maybe both. She'd never been good at nuances. In a verbal boxing ring, he was always going to win.

"I'm not sleeping with him yet, but we are in a relationship." Sophie's voice sounded stiff, even to her own ears. "I know you're upset about the situation, but I'm happy with Todd. I have had a bad time with men, and he is good to me. He is right for me." Her eyes filled, and she turned her face against the window, leaning her forehead on the cool glass. They passed through the tunnel going into Lahaina with its bright rainbow painted on the entrance, and she shut her eyes as horns honked. "I don't know how to make this okay with you."

She kept her eyes shut, and heard Jake sigh.

"I'm sorry I was an ass about it. You deserve to be happy." He patted her arm awkwardly. "I want that for you."

"Do you still want to work with me? Because I still want to work with you. But just like before, when you were making all those sexual jokes—it has to stop. Comments about me and Todd. Mean things you say. I can't deal with it." Sophie caught his gaze and blinked away the moisture welling in her eyes. "I don't know how."

"Aw, Soph. Damn it, don't cry. I can't handle that. Dirty pool." Jake blew out a breath. "We can make this work. I just never expected it to be...so hard."

All they couldn't say seemed to fill the cab of the truck. Sophie felt like they'd stood at a precipice and both of them had taken a long look into the depths—and backed away from the edge.

She tried a change of topic. "Whose truck and sports equipment are these? Pretty nice ocean sports toys."

Jake seemed to grasp it like a lifeline. "Shank Miller's. He keeps the truck here for tooling around so he looks like a local and blends better. The guy's basically a workaholic, though, always working on his music, and he has no idea how to surf or use any of this shit. So I've been taking him out, teaching him a thing or two, and providing his security at the same time."

"He's lucky to have you. And so am I." Sophie patted Jake's arm awkwardly, a gesture that mirrored the one he'd given her.

"You know me. Always with the lemons and lemonade."

Sophie didn't know exactly what he meant, but his voice was Jake again—confident, upbeat. She relaxed, smiling, and rested her head on the seat back as he told her the best places to surf on the way to Lahaina. "I'll take you and Shank out for a lesson. It'll be hilarious."

* * *

At the Kakela site, Jake reached back into the extended cab and grabbed a toolbox, setting off without a word toward the broken sensors and surveillance cams set up around the corners of the property—though vandalized, they were still Security Solutions' responsibility.

Sophie took a moment to blow out a breath, straighten her clothes and hair, and set herself right, mentally and emotionally. *Thank God they were able to work it out.* She got out of the truck and headed for the trailer.

"Welcome back to Maui." Meeting Sophie in the trailer, Pomai Magnuson was polished and stylishly dressed, as usual.

Her light embrace and gardenia perfume enfolded Sophie. "So glad we got the lunatic behind all of this, and better yet, that he gave the Hui such an amazing donation."

"I wish he had just written the nonprofit a check," Sophie said, taking the envelope holding the check out of her bag and handing it to Pomai. "I could have done without the whole hostage standoff that went on—he took his life at my hand."

"Oh my God. I'm so tactless." Pomai's face fell and she covered her mouth with a hand, shaking her head. "So sorry you went through that. I didn't mean to make light of it. I guess I just don't understand what he was trying to do, when he extracted those artifacts and then provided for them to be reburied."

"I can't discuss it," Sophie said. "I wish I could, but it's confidential. He was not a well man."

Pomai nodded. "I understand. We heard a bit from Sergeant Texeira. I'm just glad you're OK."

"Unlike Seth Mano. He got the brunt of Blackthorne's issues—to the back of his head." Sophie pulled out the familiar rump-sprung chair and rubbed her sore ankle.

"That asshole. He deserved exactly what he got." Pomai had steel in her voice. The Hawaiian woman gathered thick, lustrous black hair and wound it into a quick knot on her head, spearing it with a pencil from the desk, each movement quick and definite. "After he was killed, I ordered a full audit of all of our board and banking transactions. As president of the board, he had check signing rights. And, as I suspected, he was embezzling from the nonprofit."

"I'm sorry to hear that."

"Yeah, well. I always knew he was a scumbag." Pomai walked around the desk and picked up a folder, handing it to Sophie. "Here are your invoices and payment in full for Security Solutions."

Sophie accepted the folder. "I still have to take down the monitors in this office," she said. "It was nice to meet you, and work with you, even for a short time."

"Definitely mutual." Pomai looked out the window of the trailer and Sophie's eyes followed hers to where Jake was up on a ladder, taking down the surveillance cam. His tight black shirt and matching cargo pants made the most of his physique. "That your partner? I'm beginning to wish we'd hired him too."

"He's staying on the island for a job, so he's available in case you still need someone," Sophie said.

Pomai's rich brown eyes met hers with a twinkle and a raised brow. The other woman smiled. "Good to know. I think I'll go say hi."

Pomai lifted a hand in farewell, and Sophie sat down in front of the monitors. Disconnecting the cords and monitors and packing them into the boxes they'd shipped them in, she watched Pomai, in her tight, fitted plumeria-print sheath dress, sashay over to Jake on the ladder. The other woman shielded her eyes with a hand as she talked to him, and he descended to meet her. They appeared to be hitting it off.

A long, black hair, fallen from Pomai's bun, lay on the desk.

Sophie looked at it for a thoughtful moment, then used a piece of Scotch tape to collect the hair. She took out her phone. "Lei? Did you rule out Pomai Magnuson as a contributor to that hair on Mano's body?"

Chapter 23

Sophie sat in the observation room at the Kahului Station watching Lei and her partner, Pono, interview Pomai Magnuson the next morning. After they wrapped up the Kakela site, she stayed one more night at the condo she had been staying in. Jake had shown her around Shank Miller's compound to see the security upgrades he'd put in, and they brainstormed their roles for the rest of the job. Lei had called her late in the evening to tell her the hair she'd taken in was a match to Magnuson, and invited Sophie to observe.

The Hui director was poised and polished, as usual, smoothing another sheath dress, this time in hibiscus print, down toward her knees. Her attorney, a Caucasian named Keone Chapman, sat beside her. Pono, looking large and reassuring in a muted Aloha shirt and chinos, made an attempt at congeniality. "Always nice to see you, Pomai. Mahalo for making time to come in."

Pomai folded her arms. "Chee, brah. Nevah expec' dis from you, Pono. What, my classmate nevah can gimme one heads-up?"

"Police business, Pomai. No make pilikia—jus' answer the questions." Pono got up and turned on the recording equipment, stating the date, time, members present. Sophie frowned—she hadn't known Pomai was a classmate of Pono's—but in Hawaii, someone was always a cousin, auntie, or some kind of connection.

Lei, looking businesslike and ready for action in jeans, a black tank top and a red jacket, opened a file in front of her and fired the opening salvo.

"Tell me about your relationship with Seth Mano."

Keone Chapman held up a hand. "Why are you harassing my client? She has already answered these questions, been interviewed, and has an alibi—and the case is closed."

"It's a murder investigation. The case is never closed if new information comes to light, and it has. We are interviewing several people key to the investigation. Ms. Magnuson is one of them. Now, Ms. Magnuson, would you like me to repeat the question?" Lei asked. The window into the room faced the witnesses, so Sophie could only see the back of Lei's head, but she could read the tense alertness of her friend's body, the way even the curls on her head seemed to quiver at attention.

Pomai shrugged, playing with a couple of gold bangles on her wrist. "Our relationship was strictly business. Seth was the President of the Board of Directors of the Hui, and I am their employee. I often answered to him related to Hui business."

"Please state your whereabouts on the night that Mano was killed."

"I thought you checked my alibi?" Irritation tightened Pomai's tone. "I was at the office. My assistant was still with me. We were working. I believe you already verified this."

"What we verified was that you were indeed, at your office, and that your assistant was also there. But you were not working together, and your door was closed. She never attempted to talk to or contact you while you were inside, and there is an exterior door on the back of your office, which is located right across the street from the Kakela site. It is quite possible for you to have met Mano outside the site. Perhaps you discovered that he had sold the GPR report, and you confronted him. Words were exchanged. Perhaps he threatened you in some way, and he turned his back, and..."

Pomai Magnuson stood up. "Keone, I believe I've said all I mean to."

Chapman dug his card out of his pocket and slapped it down in front of Lei. "If you have any further inquiries, contact me first."

The two headed for the door.

Neither Lei nor Pono got up to unlock it, and Sophie felt a smile tug her mouth at the sight of Chapman's reddening face as he tugged at the handle.

"Why don't you come have a seat," Lei said gently. "We're done when I say we're done."

The two eventually returned, and Lei leaned forward and pointed her pen at Magnuson. "One of your hairs was found adhered to Seth Mano's corpse. That hair was stuck in the blood at the back of his head, the only physical evidence at all found with his body. Do you have any idea how that might have happened?"

Pomai's skin bleached to a sallow, yellowish beige. "I have no idea," she said faintly. "Oh, my God."

Chapman turned to her. "No comment needs to be your answer from here on out."

Pomai covered her mouth with a hand. "I can't believe he would do that," she murmured. "That rat bastard."

"No comment!" yelped Chapman.

"Who? Do what? C'mon, cuz, you gotta tell us. Or we goin' think you done dis." Pono's pidgin, his forward lean, his sympathetic gaze all conspired to crack Pomai's already-shattered composure—and the woman was scared.

"I made no secret of disliking Mano," Pomai said slowly. "But I had no motive to kill him—my job was secure, and even if I knew what he was up to, which I suspected, I'm just an employee. But there's someone who hates him a lot more and has a whole lot at stake—and doesn't care for me too much, either. I think that person did it, and planted my hair to implicate me."

Chapter 24

*D*r. Brett Taggart narrowed his eyes through a pale, undulating stream of smoke from the cigarette dangling from his lip as he opened the door of a run-down, third floor apartment in Lahaina. A ratty shirt and a pair of sweatpants riding low on his narrow hips told a tale of time off. "What's this about?"

Sophie peered around Lei's shoulder as her friend held up her badge. "Got some questions for you, Dr. Taggart."

"Let me get into something more appropriate."

Taggart shut the door.

"I still think Magnuson was just trying to shift the blame, point a finger," Sophie said, as Lei and Pono waited. She'd asked to come along, feeling responsible for this whole new layer of the investigation—and because she couldn't really believe that the man she'd kissed in the bar was a cold-blooded murderer.

Could she have been this wrong about Taggart?

Sophie was so bad at reading people…*she should get back behind her computers where she knew a cable from a byte.*

Several more minutes went by. Pono banged on the door with his fist. "Dr. Taggart!"

A scuffling noise came from deep inside the apartment, then the bang of a door—*or a window?*

Pono's brown eyes widened as he looked at Lei. "I think we have a runner. Let's split up and go around the building while Sophie stays and holds the position here, since she's not armed."

"Do not engage with the suspect, Sophie," Lei yelled over her shoulder, leaping toward the stairs with Pono right on her heels. "I'll go right, you go left," she directed her partner. Theypelted downward as Sophie took Pono's place. She pounded on the door. "Open up. Maui Police Department!"

No weapon. No badge. She was just a hireling with no authority, no clout, along for the ride because her friend let her come.

Sophie blew out a breath. Leaned her forehead on the door. She was so tired and so frustrated. She shouldn't have had that second beer with Jake. If she were an FBI agent she wouldn't be standing here, a placeholder, while MPD chased the suspect!

The door opened suddenly, and Sophie stumbled, falling forward, as the door was yanked wide.

"Sophie!" Taggart's eyes flew wide. "What the hell!" He shoved her out of the way, throwing her against the doorframe as he plunged past her.

No way was Brett Taggart getting away from her.

Sophie spun and bolted after him, ignoring a twinge from her ankle and yelling over the railing to Lei and Pono, "MPD! Suspect fleeing on foot!"

She chased Taggart down the stairs, and as he reached the bottom, launched herself into space to grab onto the backpack he wore, evidently what he'd been packing in some back room. Her weight, landing on him, threw him forward. Taggart stumbled and went down, sprawling on the concrete sidewalk, flattened beneath her. Sophie twisted one of his arms up behind his back in a restraint hold as she straddled his hips. "Don't you move."

"What are you doing here, Sophie? I thought you were on Oahu," Taggart panted. "My god, woman, you've got an arm on you."

"What are you trying to do, Taggart? *You idiot.* Did you really think you could get away from us?"

Taggart seemed to sag, lowering his head to the cement and breathing out a long sigh of defeat. "It was worth a shot. And you crushed my cigarettes."

* * *

Taggart rolled his big shoulders uncomfortably in the interview room, looking down at his handcuffs as if he wondered how they had gotten there.

Sophie, seated in the observation booth at Maui Police Department at Kahului Station, was beginning to feel like the dim, narrow space was a second home—except for the musty smell, which had brought on a case of the sniffles. She blew her nose on a tissue and took out her phone as she waited for Lei and Pono to come and interview Taggart. They were currently searching his backpack, and Sophie suspected it wasn't just filled with personal items.

Taggart had requested a lawyer, and Sophie observed as a very fit woman wearing a chunky amethyst necklace entered to speak with him.

She looked back down at her phone and composed a text to Connor. *"Things got hot over here with my case—we're interviewing new suspects. I'm hoping Bix gives the Miller security job with Jake to someone else, so I can come back to Oahu."*

She didn't know what else to say, how to end the sentence, so she just hit *Send.*

What did she want to say? That she missed him?

Because Sophie did miss Connor, a hollow ache that felt strange and unfamiliar, a perpetual gnaw like the bite of hunger. It wasn't even that she imagined being back in his arms; it was more that there was a sense of something missing. *Something essential.*

She shied away from what that might mean, and looked up as Lei and Pono entered the interview room.

The lawyer introduced herself as Davida Fuller. Pono apprised Taggart of his rights, and turned on the recording equipment.

"I can explain." Taggart smiled, the charming grin that Sophie remembered upon first meeting him. "I didn't kill Mano. You alibied me out before, remember?"

"Then why did you run?" Lei pinned him with her patented bad cop stare.

"You surprised me at my door, in my home." Taggart made a little shooing motion with his hand. "I need a cigarette. Any chance…"

"No chance. You ran from us, and your backpack has some very interesting contents."

Taggart shrugged.

"Your backpack was full of artifacts."

"All legit. I was transporting them for my company."

"You were stealing those artifacts, and Mano blackmailed you about it. We found your name on the blackmail list in Mano's computer."

That wasn't true. Sophie frowned. They would have been on Taggart much sooner if his name had been there.

As if to confirm Lei's provocative comment, Taggart leaned

forward and rubbed his eyes, pointing to the lawyer beside him. "Got any advice for me?"

"No comment. You say no comment. They're just fishing. They have to prove anything you don't tell them."

Taggart turned back to Lei and Pono. "Well, if you want the truth, I had a little weed in the apartment, all right? And no medical card. So, I put it in my pack along with some artifacts I was taking to the office."

"We found the weed. It's a misdemeanor. Why wouldn't you just sit and talk with us for a few minutes, instead?"

Taggart rubbed his lips. "I really need a cigarette."

"Filthy habit," Fuller said. She turned to face the detectives. "Running away is not a declaration of guilt, contrary to popular opinion."

"He resisted..."

"A private security operative who was masquerading as a police officer? My client distinctly heard her call out, "MPD" and she is not in the MPD."

Sophie's mouth went dry. She had called out MPD in order to alert Lei and Pono to Taggart's runaway; now it was being used against her.

"We think these artifacts are stolen and that's why you ran from us," Lei said. "You knew we had figured out that Mano was blackmailing you, and that you had motive to kill him."

"It was just the weed. I swear."

"No comment," Fuller said loudly. She stood up. "And now, if you don't have any further questions for my client, we'll be going."

"No you will not." Lei ignored Fuller, focusing on Taggart. "We checked with your archaeology company. The items we confiscated from your backpack were never logged in anywhere. We are placing you under arrest for the stealing of important relics from the State of Hawaii."

Fuller turned to him. "This is minor. We'll get you out on bail as soon as you have a hearing."

Taggart's cynical dark eyes widened, and real apprehension showed in them for the first time. "No. I didn't steal those artifacts. Yes, they weren't logged in, and I know how it looks. Hence the desire to hotfoot it back to headquarters and log them in."

Fuller sat down. "Do you want to tell them anything more? Because it will be used in the case against you for stealing the artifacts."

Taggart narrowed his eyes. "We both know that's just an excuse to hold me so they can search my apartment and computer, try to find something connecting me to Mano."

Lei leaned forward. "So why don't you save us all some hassle and tell us about that? I'm sure hitting him was a heat of the moment kind of thing. The man was a scumbag. Perhaps he threatened you, asked for more money? Perhaps you found out that he sold the GPR report to Blackthorne?"

"He did?" Taggart's brows drew together. "He really was a scumbag, blackmailing people. Selling out the GPR report. But I didn't know any of that. I never saw him that evening, I swear. I wish I had a better alibi, because I was alone, paddling my canoe—but it's the truth. And please, take those relics to my company and ask Peggy, our VP of Operations, to log them in. I was getting sloppy, is all, and it bit me on the ass. And now I'm done talking."

Dr. Brett Taggart folded his arms and sat back, and he really was done talking. Nothing Lei or Pono tried after that worked to get him to say anything but, "No comment." Sophie felt sad and deflated as she watched the archaeologist be led away to booking.

How had she been so wrong about him?

Chapter 25

Sophie got into her rent-a-car and headed out from Kahului Station. The Ford Fiesta had little acceleration power, exactly how she felt, thinking about the interview with Taggart. *How had she been so wrong about him?*

He'd lured her into believing in him with his jokes, with his insouciant, friendly manner.

She had helped solve the case. It was now on Lei and Pono to find evidence linking Taggart to the body more definitively.

She checked her phone. A text had arrived from Connor: *"I talked to Bix. He needs you on the Maui job, no one available to cover. I guess that we will just have to endure the separation...I miss you already, damn it. So does Anubis."* He had attached a picture of the Doberman with his head on his paws, his eyes drooping sadly, his ears comically out to the side, an expression Sophie had never seen on the alert guard dog. She snorted a laugh even as her heart squeezed.

"I miss you too." The words were inadequate to describe the empty, numb feeling that was almost a sensation in her body, an ache and a weariness that reminded her of depression, but was topped by a fillip of longing.

"Take precautions. Warn Jake about the threat against

you and stay close to him," came back from Connor.

Sophie frowned. "No," she said aloud. Jake didn't need to get any more stressed out than he already was with the Miller job. She'd be safe on that armed, alarmed compound, in a guest room next to Jake's. The last thing she needed was an overprotective man hovering and ordering her around.

Kahului was a snarl of stop-and-go traffic. Portly tourists from the cruise ships parked in the harbor made their sweaty way along the sidewalks. Motor scooters whizzed by homeless people pushing shopping carts. Other than a preponderance of pickup trucks and cars with surfboards on them, Maui's largest town could have been anywhere in Southern California—except for the coconut palm trees waving in the constant breeze along the thoroughfare.

Sophie pulled into Shank Miller's lush compound's driveway in Wailea. At the familiar stone obelisk, she told her business and was admitted.

Jake came out of the outbuilding that held the rock star's home gym. Shirtless, in loose-fitting sweats, he'd clearly been working out. He pumped a twenty-pound dumbbell as he approached her, and the noonday sun was kind to his gleaming musculature.

Following Jake out of the workout room was a six-foot tall man with long black hair past his shoulders, wiry arms covered in full sleeve tattoos, and white skin marked by a rosy flush of exertion and sunburn.

"Dude. Who is this goddess?" The man's grin was appreciative as Sophie got out of the Fiesta. A gap where a canine tooth should have been lent a piratical look to his face, an impression enhanced by the gold hoop in his ear.

"Sophie, meet Shank Miller," Jake said, gesturing to the rocker with the dumbbell. "Lead singer of the band known as Shank."

"Hello. I'm Jake's partner." Sophie shook the rocker's hand. "I'm sorry, I'm not familiar with your work, but I am pleased to meet you."

"Not familiar with my work, huh? I'll have to give you a CD."

"Thank you, but I usually listen to classical. You were away last time I came by your home. I hope Jake isn't working you too hard in the gym."

Miller flexed a ropy arm, and his tattoos rippled like fabric. "He's doing the best he can with this pasty boy from Seattle. I'm going to have a pumped-up body any day now. I've promised my manager." He winked. "Going shirtless now just scares the girls."

"Your chest is a little underdeveloped, but I'm sure there are some women who like that tortured artist heroin addict look," Sophie said.

A shocked pause, then Miller tipped his head back and laughed. "Contrary to how I appear, I've never been into drugs, but clearly I need to get back to my workout and take in a few more calories. Gimme that weight, Jake." Miller took the dumbbell and pretended to tip over from the heaviness. "This tortured artist needs feeding. Antigua!" Miller bellowed as he headed for the house, attempting the arm curls Jake had been doing. "I need food!"

Jake grinned at Sophie. "Welcome to Hale Kai when the king is in residence."

"He's funny. I like him." Sophie turned and reached in to grab her duffel bag.

"You called him a tortured artist who looks like a heroin addict!" Jake was still grinning as he led the way to their guest bungalow. "Told him his chest was underdeveloped. I'm going to have a field day using that one to motivate him in the gym." He rubbed his hands together in glee.

"Oh, I shouldn't have said that." Sophie let Jake unlock the door and usher them into the tidy, compact space inside the cottage. "It was tactless of me."

"Ya think? It was priceless. Thank you for the laughs." Jake gestured past the small living area filled with a couch and flat screen TV to a pair of closed doors down a short hallway. "Yours is on the left. Want to catch me up on your case?"

"Yes. A lot broke on the case after you left me at Kakela." Sophie chucked the duffel on the bed, but kept her large messenger bag filled with computer equipment. "Where's the security command center? I can get started setting up the nanny cam software."

Jake had put on a shirt and rejoined her in the living area. "It's inside the main house. But seriously, you can take a load off for a few. Have a beer." He popped the top on a Longboard Lager, and handed it to her.

Sophie dropped the computer case onto the couch. "I presume Mr. Miller is a casual employer."

"You presume right."

Sophie took a sip of the lager and glanced out the nearby picture window. The guest cottage faced the back corner of the property that backed up to the beachfront mansion, and Sophie looked over the high cement wall separating the houses—but in the second floor of Long's house, all the lights were on, and she could see inside.

Two husky movers were carting a piece of furniture out of the room. She pointed with the neck of the beer. "What's going on over there?"

"I checked with the realtor when I saw a lot of activity going on. Mr. Long is putting the house up for sale."

Sophie frowned, wondering at the timing. She took a sip of the lager, but she didn't really want this beer. She forced her attention back to Jake. "So they arrested Brett Taggart," she said. "After Pomai Magnuson pointed a finger at him. I feel really bad that I so misjudged him. Looks like he was stealing artifacts, probably selling them on the black market."

Jake stretched his long legs out and put his feet on the seat of the chair in front of him. "But does that make him a murderer?"

Sophie shook her head. She set the beer down. "I don't know. I'm having trouble seeing it. I'm actually having trouble seeing him as an artifact smuggler either. He seemed to care so much about the site, and his job. But he is brash and cocky, and probably doesn't like following the rules."

"You wouldn't know anyone else like that, would you?" Jake tipped his bottle toward her with a grin.

Sophie smiled. "I guess I would, now that you mention it."

She was so relieved that the tension between them had lifted. She looked around the cottage. It was small, but artfully decorated with mirrors and a few ocean landscapes that helped create an open, airy feel. Hopefully she and Jake would have enough room to stay out of each other's space.

Jake finished his beer as Sophie unpacked, putting her few clothes away in the small bureau and setting up her laptop on the desk in the corner. She returned to the main room. "Show me to the command center."

The security center of the house was located in what must have been a den at one time: an air of masculine retreat remained, fostered by a pair of deep leather armchairs, a small pool table, and a flat screen TV that took up most of one wall. But there the resemblance ended. Jake had set up a bank of monitors on a table along another wall, and they cycled through views of the property from various angles. A young Hawaiian man looked up as they entered and gave her the *shaka* hand signal. "You must be the tech expert Jake has been waiting for."

Sophie shook his hand, introducing herself. "Where are the camera nodes for the nanny cam software?"

"I was hoping you could use all of these current views and camera positions to feed in," Jake said. "It took me and Ronnie here a week to put up all of these cams and network them."

"They look good at first glance. We can use all of that, and put in more or different positions if we're not getting enough data. Where is Mr. Miller, currently?"

"In the gym." Ronnie tapped a sensor screen in front of him and pulled up one of the squares. The monitor immediately filled with a view of a panting Miller doing sit-ups, a pair of headphones wrapped around his ears.

"I have him put on a tracking bracelet as soon as he gets to Hawaii," Jake said. "We have tracking software and the video cams tuned to his signal, so we can find him anytime he's within range."

"Seems very sensible. Have you been collecting data on the household patterns for the artificial intelligence program to process, once I've got it installed?"

"I left that for you to set up, along with the program installation," Jake said. We do have a lot of stored video, but we only got the whole system going last week, so…"

"Find me a decent chair, then," Sophie said. Ronnie jumped up and fetched one of several leather office chairs rolled against the window as Sophie dug into her computer case and removed a small external hard drive.

She took out her headphones and edged Ronnie's chair out of the way, plugging both her headphones and the hard drive apparatus into the main computer bank located beneath the table. "I'd appreciate some time alone to work on this," she said, sitting down and cracking the knuckles of her good hand. "I'm sure you two can find something else to do."

"I think we've just been dismissed," Jake said to Ronnie, but Sophie was already checked out, her fingers flying on the keyboard she had appropriated from Ronnie's station as she got to work. The software went in and up with few problems, but required some adjustment of the main computer's current workflow and programs, and Sophie got lost in Beethoven and data flow.

She looked up eventually, realizing, by the low light of afternoon, that several hours had passed. She felt cramped and needed the bathroom, but didn't feel comfortable finding one in the house. She went back to the cottage, used the restroom, and stared thoughtfully out the window at the mansion next door. The activity seemed to have settled down, but the lights were all still on.

What was going on with Aki Long?

They hadn't found any association or connection between him and Seth Mano, and Lei had told her that the Hui's treasurer had been at a fundraiser dinner on the night of the murder. She stretched, lifting her arms high over her head and bending over, glad that she'd worn her usual stretch pants and tank top. She went through a quick five-minute yoga routine, and decided it couldn't hurt to have DAVID do a quick search on Long's current activities.

She plugged the Internet cable into the powerful laptop, brought in a kitchen chair, and sat down. She activated all the firewalls she could—using DAVID outside of a secure facility like the FBI or Connor's "Batcave" was taking a risk of detection, but she couldn't relax until she investigated what he was up to.

DAVID worked by assembling data and searching keywords—but she had a hard time coming up with anything besides Aki Long's name for the program to mine for. She didn't know what she was even looking for, and that felt frustrating. She set the program to data mining for anything to do with his name and Long Enterprises, his business, and then she got up and shut the bedroom door.

"What're you up to?" Jake's voice made her jump. He was standing in the doorway, and missing a shirt again.

"Just getting my personal rig going." Sophie brushed past her partner. "I have the nanny cam software set up. It's begun analyzing the video data you've collected so far, but I suspect it will need another week or so to train. I can tell you spent a while adjusting the angles and so on with the video."

"Yeah. It's a lot of trial and error during the set-up phase." Jake cleared his throat. "Shank wants to get to know you better. Commands your attendance at dinner, where he informs me he will be calorie-loading."

Sophie glanced at the clock over the cottage's mini-stove. "What time? I'd like to take a little beach walk. Stretch my legs."

"About an hour. I'm grabbing a shower. Shank made me work out hard after your insults." Jake grinned.

"Sounds good. See you in a little while." She lifted a hand as he headed toward the bathroom.

Sophie walked around the outside of the house on an artfully planted path and paused in front of the sliders looking out at the beach.

Evening had fallen, and a brilliant sunset cast a pool of glowing gold across the ocean. Sophie could see why Miller didn't want his view disrupted. The new security wall of Plexiglas panels across the front of the yard must require a lot of cleaning, but Miller still had his view. "Good solution, Jake," Sophie murmured.

Sophie glanced toward Aki Long's house. The lights were all still on, but the mansion appeared deserted. She walked down the wide veranda and across the lawn, conscious of the surveillance cameras tracking her. The Plexiglas gate mechanism was a simple one, but she could tell she would need to be readmitted to the estate grounds once she left. Sophie checked that she had her phone to call Jake to let her back in, then stepped outside the gate.

If a notification sounded inside the house, she didn't hear one—probably egress registered in the system, but it would be an unauthorized entrance that would set off alarms. The Plexiglas gate shut with a click behind her, magnetic seals catching and sealing the six-foot clear plastic wall.

Soft grainy yellow beach sand was cooling down with evening and massaged her bare feet, causing twinges in her injured ankle even with the neoprene brace she was still wearing. Sophie looked out at the view of calm blue sea, clouds touched with orange from the setting sun. She considered walking down on the harder sand by the ocean, but found herself turning right. She soon reached the metal panel gate into Long's property.

Sophie frowned—it was ajar, and opened to her gentle push. She poked her head inside. The house was lit as if for a party, but the windows were wide open, and it was deserted. A large real estate sign blared *Gonzalez Realty* in the center of the lawn.

Sophie paused to send Jake a text: *"Something's weird about Aki Long's house next door. Checking it out."* She slid the phone back into her pocket and approached the modern minimalist porch.

"Hello?" Sophie called out cautiously as she ascended the stonework steps. Like Miller's house, the bottom floor opened up with sliders to maximize the view of ocean and sky, and she could see right into the interior.

The place was cleaned out.

Why was Long leaving so suddenly?

Her pulse picked up as she tested one of the sliders. It slid open with a squeak. Sophie put her head inside. "Hello? Anyone home?"

Her voice echoed around the empty space, but the sound of waves from the surf behind her was amplified, an effect like the sound of sea in a shell.

She wiped her feet on a sisal welcome mat and walked in.

Emptiness and echoes, and light reflecting off of polished teak floors, stucco walls, and marble counters told her that the house had been a showplace in its time. Now it showed the wear and tear of the recently abandoned.

Scuff marks marred the teak floor, and gouges in the walls showed where artwork had been removed. The faucet leaked into a steel sink in the kitchen, the *drip, drip, drip* monotonous and sad.

Sophie found a realtor's card on the counter and picked it up. "Mary Gonzalez," she read aloud. She plugged the number into her phone and hit *Send.*

As the phone rang, she headed upstairs. Here the evidence of better care showed in the burnished surfaces of the few pieces of furniture left behind.

Against one wall was a gleaming koa armoire. A king size bed frame, also koa, looked skeletal without its mattress. A shadow box filled with carefully mounted bone hooks hung over the bedframe. Under a window, a leather armchair and ottoman waited for someone to occupy them, a stained-glass lamp still on.

Mary Gonzalez had a chipper, upbeat voice. "Gonzalez Realty."

"Hello. I was passing by on my evening beach walk, and saw that Mr. Long's beautiful home is for sale." Sophie broadened the British accent left over from her boarding school days.

"Oh yes. That listing is not actually on the market yet, so you're in luck."

Sophie imagined herself as one of the socialites she'd often met at her father's diplomatic parties, and spoke with the crispness of the wealthy. "I am looking to pick up another Wailea property, so tell me about the place. I've liked this house for years, but I never thought Mr. Long would sell."

"Mr. Long regrets having to let the property go at a discount, due to his rapid departure. It's only five million!"

Sophie's brow shot up—that was still high for a house in the shape this one was in. "And why is Mr. Long leaving so expeditiously?"

"Oh, I don't really know, ma'am, but he told me unexpected family business is taking him back to Hong Kong."

"Oh really? What a shame." A feather of apprehension tickled the back of Sophie's neck. *She didn't want anything to do with anyone who had connections to Hong Kong.* Assan had fingers in many pies, and informants in all sorts of places. She did not want her ex finding out where she was. "Well, thank you for your help. That is indeed a steal. Let me discuss it with my husband and get back to you."

Sophie ended the call on the woman's queries for her name, and slid the phone into her pocket, her gaze falling upon the bone hook shadow box.

The hooks were likely only replicas, arty decorations for the room. But still, they fascinated her. She approached and stepped inside the bed frame, lifting the box off the wall. Behind it, a square door outlined the presence of a wall safe. Sophie frowned, tracing the white-painted metal facing. It had a modern thumbprint lock as well as a combination dial—higher security than usual for a home safe. *What was he hiding in here?*

She walked over to the lamplight with the shadow box to see the hooks better.

"Lovely collection, isn't it?"

Sophie almost dropped the box, whirling to face the voice.

Aki Long stood in the doorway, and he was holding a weapon.

Sophie's pulse spiked as she registered everything in a flash: the weapon was a Beretta. Long's golf shirt was wrinkled and sweat-stained, his hair mussed, his face shiny with exertion and suppressed emotion—*rage? Triumph?* She couldn't read him.

"I'm allowed to shoot a trespasser on my property," Long said.

Maybe she could talk her way out of this.

Sophie set the shadow box carefully down on the seat of the chair. "I apologize, Mr. Long. I shouldn't have come over. I was setting up security next door, and..."

"I know why you came. You were poking around, looking for something to tie me to the Kakela mess."

Sophie turned to face him, keeping her eyes down, her hands demurely folded. "Oh, no. I'm interested in purchasing your home. I actually just called your realtor. Let me show you..." She slid her hand toward her pocket.

"Hands where I can see them!"

"I'm sorry. Of course. I'm not armed." Alas, that was true. "You can see that my pocket is flat. I was just going to get Mary Gonzalez's card out." She used her fingertips to remove the card and drop it. The card fluttered to the ground like a fall leaf. "I thought your home was lovely. My father is an ambassador and is looking for a retirement place..."

"Bullshit." Long looked wildly around, as if seeking an answer to his conundrum. "You wouldn't be here if you didn't have something on me. What do you have on me?" Spittle flew from his mouth. *The man was losing his composure.* The redness of his face was stress. "This is an illegal search. Anything you have found here is not admissible."

He thought she had something on him. There was something in this room connecting him to the Kakela site! There was only one thing in the room it could be.

Sophie spun and smashed her casted hand down onto the glass window of the shadow box, shattering it with a crash.

Long gave a cry and stepped forward. "I'll shoot!"

Sophie reached in blindly, keeping one hand up toward him and her eyes on Long. Ignoring the cutting shards, she grabbed one of the bone hooks, and held it high. "Hide in plain sight. A great way to conceal these priceless treasures. These are from Kakela, aren't they? Relics you stole, and some of which you sold to Blackthorne. Mano found out, and tried to blackmail you."

Long's gun hand wobbled. "You have no proof."

"But I will when I take these hooks in for Dr. Taggart to assess."

Something dark and ugly passed behind Long's eyes. "Him, Blackthorne, and Magnuson will take the fall for Mano, for the burglaries at the site."

Sophie had to provoke him into a mistake. "Let me guess. You and Mano were blackmail partners. We never did find his stash of blackmail material, and that's because you have it, probably in that safe on the wall. But Mano overreached himself and tried to sell you out. You bashed him on the head and planted Magnuson's hair on the body."

Long breathed through his nostrils heavily, his eyes darting. "So what? You've got no proof."

"I do, now that I've found this evidence," Sophie said, coiling all her energy inward, readying to attack.

"Not admissible. I know my rights." He took another step toward her. "But you're a loose end."

Long's mouth tightened and so did his finger on the trigger—

just as Sophie dove for his legs, holding the large shard of glass in her hand. The gun fired with a sound like spitting a watermelon seed, barely missing her as she drove the glass into the man's calf.

Long howled and brought the gun down toward her.

"Sophie!" Jake yelled from the top of the stairs, and Long swung his arm up and fired at her partner instead. Sophie heard a thump from the doorway as Jake fell backward down the steps.

Sophie wrapped her arms around Long's legs and used them and the floor for leverage as she flung her good leg up in a kick that caught Long's gun hand. Long lost his grip on the pistol and it arced through the air, landing on the shiny floor with a clatter. Sophie brought Long down with a grappling move, and the Asian man crashed onto the floor. She whipped the golf shirt off over Long's head and twisted it behind his back to bind his hands, then ran to fetch the fallen weapon as Long cursed and groaned.

"Jake?" She hurried to her fallen partner. He lay partway down the steps, his back to her. "Jake, are you okay?"

He wasn't okay.

Chapter 26

"Jake?" Sophie hurried down the stairs to where her partner had fallen and stepped over his body to look at him from the front. His skin was pale, and a swelling marred his forehead—but he was breathing. A round had penetrated Jake's shoulder, and blood spread across his black shirt, a shiny wetness that she was relieved she didn't have to see—the amount soaking the shirt was alarming, and she felt queasy at the sight, at the coppery smell in her nostrils, at the reality of Jake, shot, at her feet.

Sophie fumbled her phone out, dialing 911 with shaking hands, calling for an ambulance at Long's address, as she ran back up to where Long was still lying stunned, bleeding messily from his leg wound. She retrieved some curtain ties and secured Long's ankles and hands more firmly, then returned to Jake.

Jake came around and groaned as she touched his cheek. He opened his eyes. "This hurts too much to be heaven."

"Definitely not heaven. But hopefully help is on its way. I need to get you flat so I can put pressure on your wound." She looked around wildly. "Where is Ronnie?" She was proud of how steady her voice sounded, though her hands were shaking badly. "He must have heard the gunshot."

"You can call him on my phone." Jake indicated his pocket and she dug it out, scrolling to Favorites and calling for Jake's colleague's help.

Jake seemed to rally, rolling toward her and reaching up. She got under his good arm, using her leg strength to lift. She hefted him up the four stairs that he had fallen down, and he retched as she lowered him to the landing onto his back. He was ghastly pale, and his eyes looked gray as mist in the waning light—it was too easy for her to imagine a fixed stare, his color gone, his body going slack forever.

Sophie grabbed the chair's back cushion and applied it to Jake's shoulder, leaning on the wound to stanch the bleeding.

His eyes flew open and he glared at her. "Son of a bitch, that hurts!"

"Stubborn son of a three-legged goat, always jumping in without looking! You are going to get killed one day, and it will break my heart," she cursed right back, in Thai.

"You said that like you meant it," Jake whispered. "Makes me wish I understood whatever it was. But mine are better." He proceeded to flood her with inventive cursing—this time in Spanish.

Sophie smiled down at him. "Spanish is a lovely romance language and you are really mutilating it with your awful accent and common gutter slang. I prefer, for extreme cursing, to use Mandarin." Sophie let loose a stream of her favorite insults, and was rewarded by a faint smile as her partner shut his eyes.

He groped for her hand with his good one. She held it as she leaned on the pillow, using voice dial to call Lei and tell her what had happened just as Ronnie arrived, wide-eyed at the sight of unstoppable Jake felled, and Long trussed up and moaning.

It was a long fifteen minutes until the EMTs arrived, having no trouble coming into the compound with Long's gates wide open. Lei and Pono arrived shortly afterward, and Sophie left them and Ronnie to deal with Long as she followed the gurney carrying Jake across Long's yard, still holding his hand.

At the ambulance, one of the EMTs gestured to her splint. "Want us to clean that up for you?"

Sophie was dripping blood from a laceration from the glass, and had not even realized it.

She kept her eyes on Jake's as the EMT bandaged her wound while the other one hooked up IVs and monitoring equipment and prepared to put Jake into the ambulance.

"You big ox," she whispered in Thai. *"Don't you die on me."* She squeezed his hand. She felt like doing more to show him she cared, but couldn't think of anything that would be appropriate. "We have to stop doing this."

Jake nodded. "Yeah. It's getting ridiculous. I'm telling Bix we need combat pay."

"I'll be there as soon as I can get away," she promised, and he finally let go of her hand when they pushed the gurney into the ambulance.

Chapter 27

After taking Sophie's official statement of events on video, Lei asked the team to sit through a recap of the case on one of the whiteboards in Kahului Station's utilitarian conference room. Sophie held a cup of hot cocoa with both hands, letting the warmth soak in and calm her shaking hands, the sugar stabilizing her adrenaline crash, the sweet scent erasing the memory of the smell of Jake's blood in her nostrils.

"So, as you know, Long lawyered up as soon as he was treated for his stab wound," Lei said. "He claims he surprised Sophie stealing his bone hook collection and that he was within his rights to fire upon her and Jake, an additional intruder."

"He will have trouble proving that," Captain Omura said. The Japanese woman brushed at her immaculate uniform and pushed an errant strand of smooth black hair behind her ear.

"True, but his lawyer is backing him up, so that's the battle we'll be fighting. But we got a search warrant for the safe, and a safecracker is on his way. I can't wait to get my hands on all the dirt hidden in there," Lei said, the dimple in her cheek flashing in anticipation.

"He virtually admitted to the murder of Mano, as I told you,"

Sophie said. "I speculated that he was Mano's partner, and that he killed Mano for trying to extort from him, and his answer was to tell me I had no proof."

"If the blackmail materials are in the safe, we'll have a solid case. We will have a trickier time proving that he was near the body with no physical evidence but Magnuson's hair, but we can build a pretty convincing picture with the circumstantial evidence," Hiromo, the District Attorney, said from his side of the table. "Though of course, I will be counting on your testimony, Ms. Ang."

"Of course. Did you let Dr. Taggart go?" Sophie asked Lei.

"We did. His company declined to press charges on him for having the artifacts in his possession. They said they believed his statement that he had merely neglected to log them in. He's working at his lab with a partner to authenticate Long's bone hook collection. We expect those to be human bone hooks, and hopefully the archaeology team will find a way to tie them to the Kakela site," Lei said. "So. Let me take us through the case and see if we have any loose ends. Kakela was being burgled by someone looking rather haphazardly for bone hooks. Security Solutions is hired to prevent the incursions. Seth Mano's body turns up in one of the 'test unit' holes on the site, head bashed in. Only physical evidence is Pomai Magnuson's hair on his body." She looked around. "Anyone need a malasada break besides me?"

"Texeira, we've gone to heart-healthy snacks here at Kahului Station, as you well know," Captain Omura said. "I can have someone bring in some celery sticks and hummus, if you like."

"No, thank you, sir." Lei shuddered. "Anyway, Sophie found a list of blackmail victims on Mano's computer. One of the names on it was Brock Blackthorne, who had recently put in a bid on the Kakela site. We went out to his estate to question him in the matter, and he took Sophie hostage. He had been behind the burglaries, and Seth Mano had sold him the GPR report, which helped him target the artifacts he was after, including the bones of the Hawaiian queen. We were able to extract Sophie, but Blackthorne committed suicide in the process."

Sophie felt a chill pass over her skin at the memory of Blackthorne's blood pumping over the obsidian knife in her hand.

"The case appeared closed, though we weren't sure how Blackthorne had killed Mano. Then Sophie asked me to check Pomai Magnuson's hair against the one found on the body. She wasn't in the system, but we were able to obtain a sample and verify that it was her hair on the body. When we brought her in, she fingered Brett Taggart, who then fled his apartment in an attempt not to be caught in possession of artifacts that he had not logged in with his company, making him look like a good candidate for the murder." Lei paused and took a swig of her water bottle. "Am I right so far?"

Nods.

"Anyone got anything to add?"

"I never thought Taggart was the killer," Sophie said.

"Well, he's a likeable guy, but it's not a popularity contest. We follow the evidence wherever it leads, and Sophie found another lead just when we were ready to close the case again and pin it on Taggart. She went over and trespassed at Aki Long's house, uncovering evidence linking him to the bone hooks and an admission that he was involved."

"Now all we need is something from that safe on Long's wall to tie to Mano or Kakela for us to be able to make a convincing case," Pono said. "Sophie, I know you want to go see Jake at the hospital. We'll call you if there's anything you need to know."

Sophie was grateful to be dismissed.

* * *

Jake was on the fourth floor of Maui Memorial Hospital, propped up in bed, his shoulder thick with strapping.

The nurse had told Sophie to "go right in," but Jake's eyes were shut, and she hesitated in the doorway.

She'd scrolled through his phone at the scene and, after the ambulance took him away, called his mother and sisters to tell them that he'd been shot; they were on their way, and to judge by their horrified exclamations, he was well-loved.

And he should be. Jake was every inch a hero, several times over.

Sophie padded forward silently so as not to wake him, but Jake's eyes opened. Though glassy with pain meds, his gaze brightened at the sight of her. "Thought you'd never get here."

"How did the surgery go?" Sophie sat in a slick plastic chair beside the bed. "Here's your phone back." She set it on the little table beside the bed.

"They told me they got the bullet out." He pointed with his good hand to a small lidded glass jar. "Gave me a souvenir. Said I'd recover as well as could be expected, whatever that means."

"Lei will probably want that bullet." Sophie picked the jar up and shuddered at the thought of that conical gray slug being dug out of his flesh and bone. "I'm just sick that this happened to you."

"Better than the alternative."

She looked up and met his eyes.

"I'm getting tired of men taking a bullet for me," Sophie

whispered. "Men I care about. I think I need to get into another line of work."

Jake fumbled a big hand across the bedclothes and reached for hers.

Sophie didn't want to take it. *She had a boyfriend.* Jake might get the wrong idea...but she couldn't resist her partner's mute appeal. She sighed, taking his hand in her own bandaged one and leaning against the bed. "I'm so tired," she said. "What a long, horrible day."

"Come rest a while. I'm going to sleep," Jake mumbled.

Sophie scooted her chair closer, and leaned her head against the angled back of his bed, their joined hands resting on the edge. His bulky warmth soothed her, as did the sound of his breathing. Just a few minutes of rest, that was all she needed, and she'd be on her way back to her condo, after he was asleep and he didn't need her any more. It had been such a long day.

* * *

Sophie woke with a start to a touch on her shoulder. Dawn was breaking over the ocean, sun shining through a window that had shown nothing but an inky night sky when she first sat down. She was stiff and achy, having fallen asleep in that uncomfortable position for hours.

A kind, matronly face looked down at Sophie, gray eyes inquisitive. "Are you the woman who called me?" The woman whispered, pushing ash-blonde hair back behind her ears and setting a bulky purse on the floor beside the bed.

"I am," Sophie whispered, extracting her hand from Jake's and stifling a groan as she straightened up to stand, every muscle screaming. "Are you his mother?"

"Yes, I'm Janice. Janice Dunn."

"I'm so glad you're here. He will have company now." Sophie smiled and picked up her backpack as she sidled toward the door. "Tell him I'll call soon."

"Are you his girlfriend?" Mrs. Dunn sat in the chair she'd vacated.

"No, no. I'm his partner. At the security firm. We work together," Sophie stuttered, glancing at Jake, who was, mercifully, still snoring among the beeping machines. "I'm Sophie Ang."

"Oh." Mrs. Dunn's mouth turned down. "All right then. Thank you for calling me. He probably wouldn't even have told me anything happened until he was better."

"He's pretty independent," Sophie agreed. "But everyone should have company when they're injured and hurting."

Mrs. Dunn nodded, her gaze fastened on her son, and Sophie slipped out.

She found a bathroom and used the facilities, then splashed water on her face. Her complexion looked ashy and her hand ached. They were both so lucky that one, or both of them, hadn't ended up on a slab in the morgue. She gave another little shiver, and dug her phone out of her purse.

Lei had called, confirming that Aki Long's safe contained the blackmail materials they had been looking for, and that they "had him nailed." Sophie smiled at her friend's triumphant tone. "And don't bother using DAVID on him right now. We have him dead to rights, and I don't want you getting in trouble with that rogue program on our behalf," Lei ended. Sophie couldn't help but feel relieved.

Several calls from Connor showed, and even a couple of voice mails: "Are you all right? I heard Jake was shot! Call me."

Then a second one: "I'm coming over. I'm sure you're at the hospital with him. I'll be there soon."

That was three hours ago.

Sophie's pulse picked up as she strode out of the bathroom, calling Connor back, but there was no phone reception in the hospital. She hurried down the glossy, antiseptic-smelling halls into the elevator and down to the exit. She'd taken an Uber from the nearby police station, and tried another call to Connor before she summoned a ride back to her condo.

"Sophie? I'm almost at the hospital. Are you okay?" Connor's voice energized her immediately. She felt exhaustion and trauma falling away as if plugging into an electric current.

"I'm fine. I'm out at the front. Can you pick me up and take me back to my condo? Jake's resting and his mother just arrived," Sophie said, rubbing her scar distractedly.

"Perfect."

Five minutes later, Connor pulled up in a big white Honda SUV. "Security Solutions has vehicles over here?" Sophie asked, hopping into the passenger seat before he could open the door for her.

Connor put the vehicle in park, stomped on the parking brake, and gestured. "Come here. I need a kiss after that harrowing experience of worrying about you."

Sophie smiled, warmth crackling over all of her nerve endings. She leaned over and Connor caught the back of her head, drawing her in for a deep kiss that brought on a whistle from someone exiting the hospital.

They broke apart at last, and Sophie saw her smile reflected in Connor's face. She cleared her throat. "I'm so glad you're here."

"Me, too." Connor put the Honda in gear and pulled out from under the hospital's drop-off canopy. "And to answer your question, yes. Security Solutions has begun the process of opening a satellite office over here so we've shipped over a couple of these vehicles. I thought Jake told you. Anyway, we're not going back to your condo. I have something else in mind."

"Oh really?" Sophie quirked a brow.

"Yep. All you need is your bathing suit and a couple of changes of clothes. You're off for the weekend, and we're getting some serious R and R."

"What about Jake?" Sophie felt a tug of guilt and something more, something soft and longing as she looked back at the hospital in the rearview mirror.

"I thought you said his mother arrived?" Connor's blue eyes were guileless. He had no reason to be jealous of Jake, and she wanted to keep it that way.

"You're right." Sophie looked away. *Jake had his family. He'd be fine.* "I have a few things to finish for Lei and Pono, including a search I started on Long for the investigation, but I can do that on the laptop from wherever you're taking me. And where is that, by the way?"

"Surprises are the spice of life."

"I've never cared for them." Sophie tugged at her hair, arranging it over her scar.

"You'll like this one. But we have a bit of a drive, so why don't you tell me about the case, from start to finish?"

* * *

The road to Hana was one of Maui's special experiences, Sophie discovered. Two-lane, steep-shouldered, narrowing to one at various points, Hana Highway wound along the coastline in deep arcs, necessitating frequent and harrowing pullovers as cars passed each other. Waterfalls gushed every mile or two, and green jungle, blooming flowers, and vast bamboo forests decorated lush, steep bluffs above a tumbling cobalt sea. The drive is never shorter than two hours, Connor informed her, but the way Sophie and Connor did it, the route took three.

Sophie loved playing tourist, parking at every vista to pose for selfies with Connor, keeping a pair of binoculars out to look for whales, and walking to the base of each accessible waterfall to offer a leaf or a flower into the water, a tradition from her childhood.

Every mile that passed took Sophie further from the stresses and strains of the case. Telling Connor about it and the ugly revelation of Aki Long as the real criminal behind it all was a way to purge the experience from her mind and heart.

As they pulled in to the turnaround for valet parking at the famous, elegantly low-key Hana Hotel, Sophie tucked a plumeria behind Connor's ear. "Talking to you is more therapeutic than a debriefing with Dr. Kinoshita."

He grinned. "I'll take that as a compliment. I guess. But I have something a lot more therapeutic in mind."

Sophie laughed.

They carried Sophie's laptop and backpack, repacked from Miller's house, and Connor's overnight bag, into the single-story hotel built around a lava stone fountain. The bellman driving them in a golf cart through acres of open grounds planted in tropical plants pointed out a nine-hole golf course, an infinity pool and spa, a croquet field, tennis courts, and archery range, all providing possible activities. As they approached a bungalow overlooking the sea, Connor took Sophie's hand. "The idea is that we never have to leave the grounds."

"I agree with that plan," she said. Velvety green grass and palms swaying overhead framed a large, lovely cottage set on a swath of bluff overlooking the ocean. The bellman carried their bags in, showing them a full kitchen and welcome basket of fruit, flowers, and famous Hana banana bread.

Connor tipped him as Sophie walked through the big glass sliders to look out at the cobalt blue, wave-tossed sea. "I thought Wailea was as pretty as this island could get. But I like this, too."

"The east shore always gets more rain and storm action, but it has unique charms." Connor joined her at the railing. Side by side, they took in the view. Clouds whirled by, and a cormorant dipped over the ocean. Waves broke on the black lava rocks lining the nearby bay. The sound of surf filled their bungalow like a lullaby.

Sophie looked at Connor. "You brought me here to get me away from anywhere that Assan could track me."

"Yes. You must have noticed when we registered that we're Mr. and Mrs. Jones. We are hidden and off the grid for the weekend, as best as I could do. I thought that might help us both sleep better, for a little while at least."

Sophie turned fully toward him, still leaning on the railing. His sea-blue eyes were serious. He lifted a finger to trace the scar on her cheek. "I want you safe. I won't rest until he's dead."

She turned her head and caught the tip of his finger with her teeth, nipping it. "That's somehow very sexy. Thank you—even though Assan is mine to kill. I love you for saying that. For doing whatever the Ghost is doing to track him."

"That almost sounded like 'I love you.'" Heat bloomed in Connor's eyes as he slid his hand around the back of her neck and drew her closer. Their bodies pressed together, and the kiss kindled a fire in Sophie's belly. She leaned into it, pressing into him, shedding her preoccupation with work, her wounds from the past, her inhibitions.

Sophie lifted her head finally and brown eyes gazed into blue. "I love you, Connor. I've never said that before, to anyone but my parents."

"And I love you." His kiss was filled with the banked passion of a love she could not misinterpret. They shed their clothing on the way to a big bed overlooking the sea—and to the sound of breaking waves, Sophie left her past behind and embraced a future with the Ghost.

Aloha dear readers!

I want to begin by thanking a couple of archaeologists. This book would never have taken its current form if I hadn't met the dashing Sam Young at an art sale, and been captivated by his story of "a buried royal island" right in Lahaina that I had not been aware of. I wasn't sure how I was going to use this interesting information, but Sam was kind enough to show me around Moku`ula, the real site that inspired my fictional Kakela. When I asked what nefarious criminals might be after at a site like Moku`ula, he told me about human bone hooks, something I'd somehow missed in my research for the *Bone Hook* novel. Thanks, Sam, your enthusiasm inspired me!

At the site, which looks much like I described it (except there is no surveillance trailer where Sophie hangs out!), I was fascinated by the deep, square test unit holes dug by the archaeologists to determine the perimeter of the buried original island, and many other interesting aspects of their deep and dirty work (there are, truly, many off-color archaeology jokes!). When I posted online that I was thinking of developing a story around Moku`ula, a reader fan/friend, Jennifer Frey, an archaeologist currently working at the site, offered to help me with further consultation.

We met and Jennifer provided me maps and details about arcane things like the GPR report. She also told me the legend of the queen and the *mo`o*, a story we were not able to verify, but that captured my imagination as had so many aspects of the unique place. Thanks, Jennifer, for the work you do and for being such an enthusiastic fan of my work!

Many of the details of Kakela are true of Moku`ula: the site is a sunken royal island where Kamehameha held court until he moved to Oahu; it was filled in with dirt from road construction around the turn of the century; there are important artifacts buried there and the site is of great cultural significance; and it was also used as a baseball diamond for many years.

But from there, I took creative license and galloped away with it as only a crime writer can do. If you would like more information about Moku`ula, or would like to contribute to its restoration, check out the Friends of Moku`ula website.

Please forgive any errors—this is a work of fiction, and none of the characters have anything to do with anyone in real life. My intent, as always, is to shine a light on some aspect of Hawaii life and educate the public in a very broad way while telling an entertaining story. I mean no disrespect by any details I may have gotten wrong in police procedure, archaeology, or Hawaiiana.

If you enjoyed this story, *please leave a review*. They mean so much, and help other readers discover the books. Mahalo in advance for the best gift a writer can receive!

I am already plotting the next book, *Wired Dark*, which continues this storyline with an expansion of the Shank Miller case, Sophie's ongoing recovery from and confrontation with the characters from her past, and her journey into love.

Pop in and say hi and tell me what you thought on social media. I'm on Facebook, Twitter, Pinterest and Instagram!

Much aloha,
Toby Neal

Look for these titles from Toby Neal!

Mystery

Paradise Crime Series: (Sophie Ang)

Wired In (book 1)
Wired Hard (book 2)
Wired Rogue (book 3)
Wired Dark (book 4)
Wired Dawn (book 5)

Nightbird: a Jet World Novella
Rough Road: a Sydney Rye World Novella
(prequel to *Blood Orchids*)

Lei Crime Series:

Blood Orchids (book 1)
Torch Ginger (book 2)
Black Jasmine (book 3)
Broken Ferns (book 4)
Twisted Vine (book 5)
Shattered Palms (book 6)
Dark Lava (book 7)
Fire Beach (book 8)
Rip Tides (book 9)
Bone Hook (book 10)
Red Rain (book 11)
Bitter Feast (book 12)

Lei Crime Companion Series:

Lei Crime Kindle World
Assorted novellas by other authors expanding the world of
Lei Crime. Everything from stories from Keiki's perspective to
Pono as main character, Marcella crime solving, and much more!

Stolen in Paradise:
a Lei Crime Companion Novel (Marcella Scott)
Unsound: A Novel (Dr. Caprice Wilson)

Contemporary Fiction/Romance

Somewhere on Maui: (a Hawaii Romance)
Somewhere on St. Thomas (a Michaels Family Romance 1)
Somewhere in the City (a Michaels Family Romance 2)
Somewhere in California (a Michaels Family Romance 3)

Middle Grade/Young Adult

Island Fire
Wallflower Diaries: Case of the Missing Girl

Nonfiction

*Under an Open Sky: A Memoir on Traveling and the
National Parks* (coming soon*)*
Freckled: A Memoir of Growing Up in Hawaii (coming soon)

For more information, visit:

TobyNeal.net

Sign up for Book Lovers Club (perks, contests, chances to be an Advance
Reader) or just for new titles at http://www.tobyneal.net/ and receive a
FREE, full-length, award-winning novel!

About The Author

Toby Neal was raised on Kaua`i in Hawaii. She wrote and illustrated her first story at age five and credits her background as a mental health therapist with adding depth to her characters—from the villains to the heroes. She says, "I'm endlessly fascinated with people's stories."

Toby began her writing with mysteries, and has a well-established reputation in that genre. She decided to try contemporary fiction when she discovered that she couldn't write a book without including romance. "I'm a hopeless romantic and I want everyone to know what it's like to be deeply loved."

Toby lives with her family and dogs in Hawaii. Find her online at: http://www.tobyneal.net/

CPSIA information can be obtained
at www.ICGtesting.com
Printed in the USA
LVHW092305281019
635652LV00002B/158/P